The Bodyguard's Vessel

S. Rodman

Dark Angst Publishing

Copyright © 2022 by S. Rodman

All rights reserved.

No portion of this book may be reproduced in any form without written permission from the publisher or author, except as permitted by U.S. copyright law.

ISBN: 979-8-36-302278-4

Cover design by MiblArt

ALL RIGHTS RESERVED: This literary work may not be reproduced or transmitted in any form or by any means, including electronic or photographic reproduction, in whole or in part, without express written permission.

All characters and events in this book are fictitious. Any resemblance to actual persons living or dead is strictly coincidental.

WARNING: The unauthorized reproduction or distribution of this copyrighted work is illegal. Criminal copyright infringement, including infringement without monetary gain, is investigated by the FBI and is punishable by up to 5 years in federal prison and a fine of $250,000.

This book contains,

Assault

Physical punishment

Dubious consent

THE BODYGUARD'S VESSEL

Abuse

Suicide attempt

Alcohol abuse

Reference to past child abuse

Contents

1. Chapter 1 — 1
2. Chapter 2 — 7
3. Chapter 3 — 13
4. Chapter 4 — 19
5. Chapter 5 — 25
6. Chapter 6 — 31
7. Chapter 7 — 35
8. Chapter 8 — 43
9. Chapter 9 — 53
10. Chapter 10 — 59
11. Chapter 11 — 67
12. Chapter 12 — 73
13. Chapter 13 — 79
14. Chapter 14 — 83
15. Chapter 15 — 89
16. Chapter 16 — 95
17. Chapter 17 — 101

18.	Chapter 18	107
19.	Chapter 19	113
20.	Chapter 20	123
21.	Chapter 21	127
22.	Chapter 22	131
23.	Chapter 23	137
24.	Chapter 24	143
25.	Chapter 25	149
26.	Chapter 26	157
27.	Chapter 27	161
28.	Chapter 28	167
29.	Chapter 29	173
30.	Chapter 30	179
31.	Chapter 31	183
32.	Chapter 32	187
33.	Chapter 33	195
Thank You		199
Books By S. Rodman		201

Chapter One

Finally, I heard signs of movement from my client's bedchamber. The staff had been right about how late Lord Eban du Fray started the day.

I put my tablet down, stood up, and straightened my dark suit. First impressions counted.

I glanced over the neatly laid breakfast the staff had just laid out and wondered if it was the smell that had woken him.

Suddenly the bedroom door flung open, and I stared, managing just in time to stop my jaw from literally dropping as my gaze took in the most gorgeous man I had ever seen.

His long golden hair was all loose and disheveled, his lips plump. Storm gray eyes regarded me sleepily from a face that was pure perfection. All flawless skin and high cheekbones.

That creamy, flawless skin was all over. His red silk robe was open, revealing everything. Toned chest, pink nipples, firm stomach and a pretty cock. There wasn't a single hair on his body anywhere.

My gaze continued to drift downwards, taking in long shapely legs. I pulled my attention back up to his face and found him smirking at me. Clearly enjoying the way I was looking at him.

He leaned languidly in the doorway and gave me the once over. He smelled of alcohol, drugs and sex, but underneath that, a delicious scent all his own.

"Hi Handsome, I'm guessing you are the reason my ass is delightfully sore this morning."

His voice was like syrup, running a smooth, rich caress over my soul.

Reluctantly, I coughed and pulled myself together.

"No, I'm Bastion, your new bodyguard."

His gray eyes flashed in alarm and he jumped to attention, quickly covering himself with his robe and looking down as he tied it with trembling hands.

"Keeper and chastity belt, more like," he muttered snidely. But I could smell his fear.

"I don't care what happened last night, it wasn't my job then. I'm not going to tell your husband."

He glanced up at me then, with surprise and uncertainty in his gray eyes. But he said nothing, merely made his way to the breakfast table and sat down.

"Why did he choose a wolf shifter?" he asked.

I was impressed he could tell. Not all humans could. Even those with magic.

I shrugged, "Your husband thinks even you wouldn't sleep with a dog."

Eban made a noise of disgust as he poured his tea. Whether it was directed at his husband or the idea of sleeping with a shifter, I couldn't tell. I told myself it didn't matter. I was there to keep him safe and stop him sleeping around. Nothing else.

"So, I take it you're an omega?" he said sweetly.

My wolf bristled, and my shoulders stiffened. I was over six feet tall, broad with muscles I worked hard to achieve. I had a presence people found intimidating. I was most definitely not an omega.

Gray eyes watched me with an amused twinkle. He was trying to rile me. I took a deep breath and sat down.

"Yeah, that's right. I'm an omega," I said calmly, with no trace of sarcasm.

Eban spluttered on his tea, stared at me in surprise, and then threw back his head and laughed. A rich musical peel of a laugh that flipped my stomach over and stirred my cock.

He grinned at me, eyes sparkling. "I think I'm going to like you Bastion."

I couldn't help but return his grin. *I think I'm going to like you too.* I thought, but managed not to say it.

Fuck.

This wasn't going well at all. It was turning into a complete disaster. Maybe it wasn't too late to turn the job down and get the hell out of there. But then I thought of the huge sum of money I had been offered. It would be ridiculous to walk away from that.

Eban took another sip of his tea, his gray eyes meeting mine over his cup. For some reason, I could not look away. Deep inside of me, my wolf side whined.

The money. I was staying for the money. Nothing else. I was a professional and I could control myself. It didn't matter that desire for Lord Eban du Fray had hit me like a truck. I'd just have to ignore it. I could do anything I put my mind to.

I cleared my throat. "We need to go through some things. All excursions need to be pre-approved by me. You do not go anywhere without my permission. You do not go anywhere without me."

Eban sighed heavily. "You are not my first bodyguard, I know how it works."

"This is the first time you have had me as a bodyguard," I said sternly, putting all the authority of my alphaness into my voice. I wanted to see his eyes widen, his face pale as he realized I was not someone to be messed with.

Eban rolled his eyes dramatically and reached for a croissant. He buttered it with long eloquent fingers and ignored me completely. I'd never been so utterly dismissed in my life.

The little brat. My inner wolf wanted to growl at him and make him bare that long slender throat to me. I wanted to place my teeth on his skin and taste his submission.

"I'm going shopping today," said Eban calmly before taking a bite of his croissant.

I shook my head to clear it of all its errant thoughts. I needed to focus on the here and now. Eban wasn't a shifter, I did not need his submission. He was my charge, who I needed to superficially treat as my employer. Though we both knew I was really there to keep him in line. His husband felt he needed that, far more than he needed protection.

Eban raised one perfect eyebrow. "No?"

I fought my damn blush. That wasn't what my head shaking had been about.

"Not without giving me a full itinerary," I said gruffly.

He leaned back in his chair with his tea and grinned at me. Then he proceeded to rattle off a long list of high end clothing shops.

"That's a lot of shops," I commented when he finally stopped.

I was feeling exhausted just thinking about it. And a bit faint. Trailing after him all day was going to be hard work.

"Autumn is nearly here, darling. A whole new season to dress for," he informed me brightly as his eyes sparkled.

"How much money are you allowed to spend?" I asked.

I didn't remember seeing a figure in the briefing and the thought of having to keep tabs on his spending was daunting. Was it one of the ways I was supposed to keep him in line? I hurriedly opened up my tablet and skimmed through all the briefing notes I had been given.

"My wonderful husband gives me a generous allowance, you don't need to worry your handsome little head about it," said Eban. And he gave me a very flirtatious wink.

My stomach flipped over and my throat tightened. I knew he was going to flirt with me. I had been warned about it. It was literally part of the job description and why I had got the job. I had assured Hyde that I would never be interested in a human. It was fine. I could do this.

I ignored Eban and continued scrolling through my notes. Finally, I found the section about his allowance. It was very generous. My eyes watered at the figure. It was a crazy amount of money, but the fact the notes stated he had no way of accessing any other funds was unsettling. He only had what his husband deigned to give him. It didn't seem very fair. But they were humans and mages and it was a marriage of convenience and none of my business.

Besides, It wasn't like Eban was going without. Pushing the thought firmly from my head, I started Googling some of the shops Eban had rattled off. I highly doubted any of them would be located in a hive of villainy but I was a damn good bodyguard and I was going to do my job well.

"What time did you want to leave?" I asked.

He shrugged as he poured himself another cup of tea. "In a couple of hours."

"It takes you that long to get ready?"

"Oh darling, it's flattering you think I can just wake up looking this good."

I stared at him. I had no idea what to say to that. I had just seen him wake up looking that damn good.

His gray eyes sparkled at me, and he smirked. The little shit knew exactly what he was doing.

"I'll go tell the driver and make preparations," I said, trying not to stammer and trying to get to my feet with grace.

I felt his eyes on me and knew he missed nothing. I strode out of the room and told myself I wasn't scrambling away. He gave me a long languorous wave and my gut clenched.

Being Lord Eban du Fray's bodyguard was going to be hell.

Chapter Two

Being Lord Eban du fray's bodyguard was definitely hell. Seven hours into the job and my salary that had seemed obscene when it was offered to me, now seemed like a joke.

He was just a brat. Demanding yet effortlessly charming. Everyone tripped over themselves to please him wherever we went, and I was sure it wasn't just because he was filthy rich. He could just wrap people around his little finger, and for some reason watching him lavish his attention and charm on people was making me grind my teeth until my jaw hurt from clenching.

He ignored me, apart from to regally indicate that I was to carry his new purchases. It was how everyone treated bodyguards. I was used to being invisible. I had no idea how he managed to make it so annoying.

I followed him into yet another shop. Laden down with all his bags like I was a glorified pack horse. A sea of white marble greeted me. It was another one of those stupid shops were you couldn't even see any clothes on display. I dropped all the bags by the hideous purple sofa that was the only thing in the room. An assistant in an incredibly tight fitting suit appeared out of a door that blended seamlessly into the white walls.

"Lord du Fray!" he beamed gleefully, literally clasping his hands together. "What a delight! Champagne?"

"Of course Chivers, there is always time for champagne," answered Eban.

Chivers clapped his hands, presumably as an order to someone lurking unseen within the walls. Eban flopped down onto the overstuffed sofa, somehow managing to land in a sprawl that looked both completely decadent and extremely enticing.

"How have you been, Chivers?" Eban said brightly.

Trust him to be on name terms with a shop assistant of a stupidly expensive clothes shop. And how the hell was Eban not flagging? We had been shopping for hours and I knew he had been partying last night. Where the hell did he get his stamina from?

"Oh, very well thank you, my lord," said Chivers, and I felt my lip raise up in a snarl at the obvious fawning.

Eban seemed to lap it up. As if he hadn't already been fawned over enough today. Another assistant appeared with a whole bottle of champagne in an ice bucket, on a silver tray with just one glass. I frowned. Eban had already had more than a few glasses of champagne at the other shops we had been in. Drinking an entire bottle did not seem like a good idea.

The assistant unfolded legs from the tray like a magician and placed the newly created table next to the sofa within easy reach of Eban. The man then popped the cork with a flourish, filled the glass before returning the bottle to its ice bucket and stepping back with a little bow.

Eban picked up the glass. "Thank you, my dear," he said warmly to the assistant as he gave him his full attention.

The assistant flushed and bowed again. He was young and good looking with a mop of dark curls and a smart suit that showed off a very athletic body. I frowned.

"As you know my lord, this autumn's colors are vermilion and dove, which you have the perfect coloring to pull off exquisitely. May I suggest Jacobs' latest line?" gushed Chivers.

Eban sipped his champagne. "Indeed," he agreed graciously.

Chivers beamed and clapped his hands again and the other assistant scurried off.

I stood behind the sofa and hid my sigh. My new fancy shoes were hurting my feet and I would have loved to sit down. But it didn't seem the end of the day was anywhere in sight.

The cute assistant reappeared, but he had changed his clothes. I blinked as I realized he was going to model them. He walked up to Eban with a flawless catwalk walk, shimmied a perfect turn and sauntered out again, presumably to change into the next outfit.

The side door opened again, almost as soon as it had closed, and a cute blond boy pranced out. I slid my sunglasses back on and crossed my arms. Watching cute twinks strut about would not be a terrible way to spend some time.

The blond and the brunette took turns to glide out in different outfits. I was starting to really enjoy myself when Eban suddenly sat up.

"Oh! I like that one. Let me try it on."

Chivers sprung into action. Another hidden door opened revealing a large changing room bestrewn with red velvet and mirrors. Eban sauntered into it. I followed him.

"Going to watch me change?" he asked with a sweet smile.

I nearly flinched, it was pretty much the first time he had acknowledged my presence all day. I scowled back at him and prowled around the room, checking behind the red velvet drapes. Once satisfied there was no one hiding in there or any other secret doors, I strode out, just as Chivers was hanging an outfit on the rail.

I took up my position outside the changing room door and tried not to glower at the shop assistants. A few minutes later, the door opened very slightly. Eban popped his head out and gestured at the brunette.

"Be a sweetie and help me with this zip?"

The brunette flushed and scrambled forward. I stepped in front of him, causing him to nearly run into me. He looked up and paled.

"No," I said but it came out more of a growl.

No way was this model going into a changing room alone with Eban. I'd seen the way Eban had looked at him.

"I'll do it," I explained as I stepped into the changing room, shutting the door in the brunette's face.

I turned around to find Eban giving me a long, cool look that I couldn't interpret. Whatever it was, it raised goosebumps on my skin.

Without saying a word, he turned around and presented his back to me. I stepped up close, swallowing noisily over the sudden lump in my throat. His long golden hair was in the way so I gently picked it up and placed it over his shoulder, resisting the urge to bring it to my nose and inhale. He smelled incredible. I forced my attention to the zip and my gaze fell onto the creamy skin of his naked back. I'd seen him more or less naked the first time I had ever laid eyes upon him. There was no way I should be so affected by seeing his back.

My cock didn't get the memo though, and swelled almost painfully fast. Thank heavens he was not a shifter and couldn't scent my arousal. That would have been mortifying.

My fingers fumbled on the zip, accidentally brushing against his warm skin. He shivered, but I was probably just imagining it. I slid the zipper up slowly. It was good quality and heavy. As well as being a tight fit. Or maybe I was prolonging the moment.

I watched his pale smooth skin disappear under the gray cloth. There were faint scars on his back. I wanted to touch them. Trace the slight lines, to see if they were ridged. I was not surprised to discover he was kinky. It seemed fitting. I imagined him allowing me to flog him, and I closed my eyes as if that could banish the mental images.

The zip was done but neither of us moved. I was standing close enough to breathe down his neck. I could see the tiny blond hairs on his skin moving as my breath trailed over him. He had to be feeling it. Any second now he was going to say something cutting or try to seduce me.

His scent filled my mind, and his body heat seeped into my own. I'd never been so acutely aware of anyone in all my life. He was scant inches away from me, yet I could not touch him.

But maybe I should? I had never wanted anything more, and I was quite sure he wanted me to. Temptation surged and some small, still functional part of my brain lamented that his allure had fully caught me.

I scrambled back, as if mere distance could save me. He looked over his shoulder and there was surprise in his beautiful gray eyes. I blinked and it was gone, replaced with a sardonic look to match his grin.

"Thank you," he drawled. Teasing, mocking. Knowing full well what he had done to me.

I nodded mutely and fled the room.

Why had he been surprised? Was he that vain? That used to people being unable to resist his charms? I drew in a shuddering breath. That wasn't vanity, that was experience. I doubted many people had ever successfully broken free from his spell. I tried to feel proud that I was one of them but instead I just felt morose. Like I had just made a terrible mistake that I was going to regret for the rest of my days.

Chapter Three

Eventually Eban finished shopping. I struggled to carry all the bags to the car. I had to waddle like a penguin. If anyone did attack him, I'd be screwed. Completely hampered by all the bags in my hands. I made a mental note to bring a footman or two next time Eban went shopping. I had a horrible feeling it was an activity he liked to do often.

The driver opened the door for Eban and the little brat slid gracefully into the car without so much as glancing at me. The driver inclined his head politely then shut the door. Finally, coming round to open the trunk of the car so I could deposit my heavy load.

He flashed me a quick grin as he helped me stow all the bags securely. I could just imagine Eban throwing a fit if something toppled over and got creased. I did not want to have to deal with that.

"You know, all these shops deliver right?" chuckled the driver.

I froze, completely speechless. The little brat.

"He normally just waltzes out and the shops bring the new stuff to the house in a couple of hours."

The driver gave me a friendly pat on the shoulder and then went on his way. Shaking my head, I did one final check of the bags.

Task completed, I jumped into the back seat next to Eban. I kept my sunglasses on. The last thing I wanted was him to see how stressed out and frayed I was. He couldn't know how much he had got to me. But he ignored me completely and stared out of the window instead.

The driver pulled away smoothly. The thought of soon being in my new home was nearly making me giddy with relief.

I watched Eban as he stared out of the window for a while. Something about the sight was odd and it niggled at me. Eventually I figured it out. And it pushed most of my annoyance away.

"Why aren't you going on your phone?" I asked.

Was he having problems online? Was there a stalker or some threat I needed to know about? Eban was young, human and glamorous, yet I hadn't seen him on his phone at any point during the day. It could just be that he was prone to car sickness, but he hadn't got his phone out whilst we were shopping either. Surely trying on new outfits in exclusive shops was prime selfie material.

"I'm not allowed to have one," he said softly without turning to look at me.

I blinked in surprise. That seemed unfair. Had his husband decided that in an effort to stop him conducting affairs? It seemed like very controlling behavior to me. But it was none of my business.

My only business was to keep him safe and stop him sleeping around. I had a feeling those words were going to soon turn into a mantra.

As soon as we pulled up outside the house, a flurry of footmen came to take the bags from the car and install the new purchases safely in Eban's rooms. I trailed behind the entourage until we arrived in Eban's private quarters. The valet appeared and took over arranging the new clothes being hung in the huge walk-in dressing room. I turned around and left them to it. Sloping away to my own tiny room, next to Eban's bedchamber.

I sat on the bed, yanked off the painful shoes and flopped backwards with a weary sigh. Peace and quiet at last. No more stupid shops and fawning staff. No more of Eban's divine scent washing over me. No more watching his golden hair shimmer in the light or seeing his slender body move with feline grace. I rubbed my eyes as if I could clear all the images out of them. But they kept coming until my mind decided to fixate on the sight of the soft pale skin of his back disappearing under the zip.

I groaned. I was so screwed.

I allowed myself to rest for a couple of hours until it was early evening. Eban was home, there wasn't too much mischief he could get up to, and the last time I had seen him, he was fully occupied in bossing the staff around in putting away his outrageous amount of new clothes.

However, I eventually had to admit there might be a slight possibility I was hiding. With a groan I slipped on a comfy pair of shoes and went to check on him. Except I couldn't find him. He wasn't in his rooms. Or the dining room. I looked in the library and the various reception rooms. I even checked the ballroom. I passed the butler on the stairs and nearly asked him, but that would mean confessing I did not know where my charge was. What kind of bodyguard lost their charge on the first day?

But I was running out of places to look. The house was in Mayfair, in the middle of London. There were no gardens for him to be wandering around in. Surely he wasn't in the staff quarters? Had he eloped to some broom closet with a member of staff? My pace quickened and my hands balled into fists at the thought. It riled me because my professional pride was at stake.

I stopped stomping along and forced myself to take a deep breath. His scent drifted tantalizingly everywhere. Stronger in some places than others, but as large as the house was, it was his home. His scent was imbued everywhere, though not as deeply as I would have expected. Then I remembered Hyde saying that he had only bought the house a few months ago.

Eban's scent hadn't had time to sink into the fabrics. The house was going to smell amazing when it did. Shaking myself from my rambling thoughts, I retraced my steps back to his rooms and then set out to follow the freshest trail of his scent.

Trying not to sniff too obviously, I made my way down a hallway to an unassuming door. Opening it revealed a flight of stairs going up. I stared in confusion at it. I was on the top floor of the house.

Climbing them took me to another door. This one opened up to reveal the roof. All decked in neutral wood. Dotted with raised planters containing small trees. The sounds and smells of London at night bombarded my senses. As did the view of all the twinkling lights of the city stretched out before me.

I walked around a planter and a good sized infinity pool came into view. The water lit a vibrant blue. Eban was swimming in it with swift sure strokes, his head down.

I drifted closer. He reached the glass edge of the pool then turned around with such grace I wondered if he was entirely human. As he swam closer to me I saw he was naked. I cast my gaze around the side of the pool but I only found a discarded towel. All those clothes and he decided to prance around naked.

He saw me and stopped swimming. Regarding me with an unreadable expression. Water dripped down his face and over his shoulders as his wet hair clung to him in a smooth, perfect sheet. He looked damn good wet and naked.

"I didn't know where you were," I snapped.

He shrugged. "Didn't know you wanted to follow me everywhere like a lost puppy."

My shoulders stiffened at the exact same time as he winced. He swam the last few feet up to me, gripped the edge of the pool and looked up.

"I'm sorry," he said earnestly. "I didn't mean to be speciesist. It's a stupid expression that slipped out of my mouth."

He stared at me intently as if he was genuinely concerned he had hurt my feelings.

"It's fine. I've had worse," I said.

His gray eyes seemed to be trying to read my soul to check I really was okay. His concern was flattering. As well as surprising.

"I'm sorry you have had to put up with such assholes," he said as he finally released me from his gaze.

He hauled himself out of the water to stand before me in his full, wet, naked glory. The sight of all that water streaming down the contours of his perfect body short circuited my brain.

"Towel, please," he said smugly.

With a start, I roused myself and grabbed the towel and thrust it at him. I was quite certain my mouth had been literally hanging open. There probably had been drool. I surreptitiously wiped my mouth as he tied the towel around himself.

I thought I might have got away with it, but the salacious wink he gave me as he passed told me otherwise.

My stomach flipped over. I needed to get a grip. Lusting after Eban was one thing, letting him know about it was another. It took unprofessionalism to a whole new level. Besides, it really wasn't as if his ego needed any help at all.

I followed him inside, as I told myself that was the last time Lord Eban du Fray was going to know he had any effect on me at all.

Chapter Four

My room was small but perfectly pleasant. It was situated right next to Eban's, with only a thin wall dividing us. I liked the arrangement, it meant I'd hear any night time intruders. Though, I was fully aware that Hyde's intention was for me to hear any night time visitors. It wouldn't surprise me if Eban was that blatant. Hopefully, he wouldn't try that with me around. Dealing with that would be hell.

I lay in my comfortable bed and listened to Eban getting ready for his. I tried not to imagine him getting undressed. It was surprising he wasn't burning the midnight oil, but then again he had a late one the night before and an exhausting day of shopping. And I was here now, to stop him from getting up to no good. There was no reason for him to stay up late.

A fact I was pathetically grateful for. I was longing for sleep. Niggling thoughts of being old enough that a young human could outdo me in stamina plagued me until I finally fell asleep.

Soft sounds woke me, coming from next door. My first thought was that Hyde had come back early from his business trip. Groaning, I put my hands over my ears. Listening to Eban fucking his husband was my idea of hell. But then I realized I couldn't smell Hyde at all.

Had the little shit brought someone to his bed after all? Cautiously, I got out of bed and padded to the door that connected our rooms. Opening it silently I observed the sight before me. Moonlight streamed in through the tall windows, turning the elegant white drapes that hung open to silver. The large fourposter bed was also painted in moonlight. Eban was a small huddled shape under the covers, alone in the bed.

He cried out again. A sound of such fear and pain, I was moving before I realized I had decided to. I climbed up onto the bed and placed a hand on his shoulder. He was on his side, facing away from me but at my touch, he turned immediately. I caught a glimpse of a slither of moon-tinted death, then a very sharp dagger was pressing against my throat.

Eban's eyes were full of nightmares and fear. I could see my own death in them. He had only known me a day, he wasn't going to recognize me.

My lungs froze, and my heart stuttered. Adrenaline surged throughout my body, impotently. There was nothing I could do. His dagger was against my jugular. A tiny flick of his wrist and my life blood would pour out, far faster than my shifter strength could heal.

Grudgingly, I was impressed. It had been many, many years since anyone had gotten the better of me.

Eban slowly blinked and his eyes cleared, the nightmare fading from his eyes to be replaced with recognition. Suddenly the dagger disappeared, as abruptly as it had arrived.

Our gazes locked, as I stared down at him. I was stupidly flattered that he had recognized me, in the middle of the night, half-asleep and startled from a dark dream.

"You were having a nightmare," I said with a calm I did not feel.

Not a single muscle on his face moved. "Get used to it."

Silence stretched. I did not know what to say to that. So I changed the subject.

"Would your husband be pleased if you greeted him that way?"

A tiny wince. "My husband would not be climbing into my bed in the middle of the night."

"He is your husband!" I gasped in shock before I could stop myself. If I was Eban's husband, I'd be climbing into his bed every night. I wouldn't even have separate beds in the first place.

Eban's beautiful eyes narrowed and a sneer spread across his face. "He is my master and I am his vessel. He takes me only when he requires my magic. And he does that at civilized times."

I stared hopelessly, completely lost for words. That sounded cold. Cold and awful. Objectively, I knew about human mage culture. I knew Hyde had married Eban simply so he could drain his magic. Magic that Eban grew and absorbed within himself but was unable to wield. But hearing Eban speak about the reality of it, was shocking.

Anger filled his eyes, and I realized I was probably giving him a very pitying look. Carefully, I schooled my features into something more neutral.

I was powerless to do anything about an unhappy marriage but there was more immediate help I could offer.

"Do you want me to stay?"

He gave me a very suspicious look. "Why?"

"Because you just had a nightmare, you might not want to be alone."

"Why not?" he asked with a look of complete bewilderment on his face.

My heart clenched, and I had to fight to keep my expression blank. Had he really never had anyone comfort him before? Had no one ever taken care of him? Helped him? It was an awful thought. I had to remind myself that humans were different from shifters. They didn't have packs. They never slept in big puppy piles all together because touch was nice. They rarely had each other's backs. It sounded lonely and cruel.

I wanted to curl up with Eban. Make him the little spoon and let him feel warm, safe and protected. But I had a sinking feeling that he would never let me.

Dimly I realized he was still waiting for an answer.

"It might be comforting to have someone here."

He stared at me as if I was speaking gibberish. Confusion and annoyance in his gray eyes.

"If you want to fuck me, just say so," he said, with snide condensation dripping from his tone.

I flinched at his words, physically recoiling away. Was that what he thought of me? That I was an animal that only thought with his cock? I had wanted to help him, soothe him. His sleep tousled hair and the smell of his fear had brought out my alpha instincts to care for those more vulnerable than me. There had been nothing sexual about it.

Except I did want to fuck him. To take him, to have him writhing and moaning beneath me, lost in pleasure I was giving him.

Eban throwing my desire in my face in a moment when I had been being decent, with nothing but honest intentions, stung.

I stormed away from his bed. Anger seething from me. He was such a brat. He was manipulating me, trying to wrap me around his little finger. Using my growing feelings for him as a weapon against me.

"Why the hell would I want to fuck you?" I spat. "Your body is beautiful, but I can see how ugly you really are."

His eyes widened and the look of shame that flowed across his face, made my gut heave as if someone had kicked it.

I turned on my heels and fled back to my bed. Refusing to feel guilty. I had done nothing wrong.

Chapter Five

Hyde returned from his business trip the next day. I stayed away from the couple. I'd already reported to Hyde via email. He knew there were no incidents to report. Aside from flirting with me a little, Eban had done nothing wrong. There had been no threats to his safety, but I knew Hyde wasn't really worried about that.

For the thousandth time, I wondered why I had taken this job. Policing someone's chastity was shady as hell. It was twenty twenty-three for heaven's sake. If Eban wanted to sleep around, surely that was between himself and his husband?

Then I recalled the money that had already slid into my bank account. The thought of it filled me with avarice, and that flooded me with shame. Was I a bad guy now? Ignoring morals for the sake of cold hard cash?

Hiring me to keep tabs on Eban was perverse. But Hyde was clearly rich enough to do whatever the hell he liked. He was human, wealthy and a mage. It was an obnoxious combination. One I was happy enough to work with because it made me richer. I groaned in dismay, I was doomed.

An image suddenly flashed across my mind again. Eban in the moonlight, impossibly tiny in that giant bed. That look on his face as I stormed away. My heart missed a beat and my throat tightened. It was for the best, I told myself. He wasn't going to play games with me and flirt anymore. I'd be able to concentrate on my job.

For some reason my inner wolf was deeply unhappy at that thought. I ignored it. The moon was nearly full, my wolf was likely just unsettled and restless because it needed to go for a run.

Until then, I needed to pull myself together. Eban and Hyde were going to a large dinner party tonight. I had work to do.

The host's house was not as fancy as Eban's home. I was getting the idea that Hyde was filthy rich even by their social circle's perspective.

The venue might not be up to Hyde's standards, but there was still plenty of marble and chandeliers. Staff greeted the guests at the door and hurried away with any coats that people had chosen to wear in the mild evening air. There were a few other bodyguards in attendance and I exchanged polite nods with them.

Eban's arm was looped over his husband's and he chatted brightly with the hosts. He looked beautiful in his well-fitted tux and happy to be on his husband's arm. Maybe their marriage was not as cold as I had imagined.

I trailed behind the couple as they slowly made their way deeper into the house, stopping to talk to everyone along the way. All day, Eban had paid me no heed at all. Ignoring me more thoroughly than the furniture. It should have been a relief, but as the day wore on my ridiculous yearning to have him just glance at me was only growing stronger.

I was not there to be seen or acknowledged. A good bodyguard was supposed to be furniture. Unobtrusive. Unnoticed until they were needed. Eban ignoring me shouldn't even be registering on my radar. I had no idea why it was annoying me so much.

I'd been a bodyguard for five long years. To a selection of snobby pricks who ignored me. Maybe this was just the straw that broke the camel's back.

It could be a sign it was time to phone my brother and ask if I could come home. Five years after our father's death, five years for the pack to settle down with their new Alpha, could well be long enough. A second alpha in the pack might not cause too much friction now.

A soft bell chimed and the guests all made their way to the dining room. The long table was huge, there had to be a hundred guests. The starch white table cloth gleamed and each place setting was festooned with a ridiculous amount of silver cutlery.

Hyde took his place near the head of the table. Eban was seated several places down. That surprised me. A quick glance around confirmed that several other couples were also separated. It must be some mage culture thing. I took up position behind Eban, standing with my back pressed against the wall. Hands clasped in front of me. And settled in for a long boring evening.

The dinner began, and I watched Eban charm everyone around him until they were all eating out of the palm of his hand. It was quite a skill. I listen for a while before tuning out the conversation and letting my mind wander. A good bodyguard doesn't eavesdrop.

My attention snapped back to Eban when he nearly choked. I had missed whatever was said to make him laugh so abruptly. He grabbed his glass of white wine and washed his food down, recovering quickly. I was almost disappointed at not having to do the Heimlich maneuver.

The middle-aged man sat opposite Eban spoke up. "Not like you to gag on a mouthful, du Fray."

Anger coiled through me. Instant and fierce, but Eban just laughed. A rich musical laugh.

"Thank you for your concern, your grace. But I always swallow."

The man, presumably a duke, judging by Eban's address, just stared back at him wide eyed. Everyone within earshot sniggered. Then the duke flushed and I just could tell that Eban had given him one of his naughty winks. A strange mix of pride and jealousy swirled through me. Quickly followed by dismay. I should not be letting Lord Eban du Fray get under my skin so completely.

I tuned out the conversation again and decided to retreat by having a little nap. There was a reason bodyguards wore dark glasses. With a little practice, it was possible to snooze whilst standing and without drooling. Hopefully, I could doze the rest of the evening away and make it pass quickly. Then I could escape to the sanctity of my own room, away from Eban.

Closing my eyes, I tried to think of happy thoughts or to pull up happy images. But all my mind wanted to supply me with was Eban. Sighing in defeat I opened my eyes to discover his chair was empty. I frowned. I must have dozed off without realizing. Anxiety and unease rushed through me. My first thought was to rush off and search for him but I calmed myself down. He was allowed to go to the toilet. I'd give him five minutes and then I'd go looking for him.

A movement caught my eye. The duke was leaving the table. I watched him suspiciously. He was allowed to go to the toilet too. I looked at my watch. Five minutes and then I'd go check.

I made it to three minutes and fifteen seconds before I was striding away to find the toilets. It didn't take me long. I stood outside the locked door and breathed in Eban's divine scent along with the scent of another man and the potent smell of arousal.

I pushed the door open, my shifter strength snapping the lock easily. The duke had Eban pressed against the wall, both their trousers were around their ankles.

The duke jumped and whirled to face me. He flushed a spectacular shade of red, hurriedly pulled up his pants and fled without a word. I watched him go. Battling with my wolf to not chase after him. I turned back to Eban to find him calmly tying his belt as if nothing had happened. His head was down, blond hair covering his face so I couldn't see his expression.

"Did he get it in?" I heard myself snarl.

He flinched and shook his head. Then he walked over to the sink and washed his hands. I just stared, speechless, incredulous. He took a comb out of his pocket and started tidying his hair.

"You're unbelievable," I snapped.

His gray eyes met mine in the mirror, and he winced. Two spots of color appearing high on his cheeks. He quickly dropped my gaze. Gave himself one last check in the mirror and brushed past me, heading back to the dining hall.

Mutely, I trailed behind him. He took his seat and resumed his conversation nonchalantly. But there was something subdued about him. He seemed to lack his earlier exuberance and sparkle.

My phone hummed against my chest. It was a message from Hyde. 'Was he up to no good?' I typed my reply quickly. 'Yes. with the duke sitting opposite him.' I slipped my phone back into my jacket pocket.

Anger seethed through me. Eban had slipped away from right under my nose, to fornicate with the vile duke. In a frigging toilet of all places. How dare he. His husband was yards away, did he really think he would get away with it? What the hell was he playing at?

The thought of the duke's hands on him made my skin crawl and my wolf snarl. I did not like it one bit.

The look he had given me in the mirror haunted me. I replayed it in my mind, trying to puzzle it out. He hadn't looked smug. Or amused. Or dismayed at being caught. In fact, the only thing I could really discern was shame. I swallowed thickly. Shame at being found out, surely?

I saw again the way he had been against the wall, the duke pressing up against him. The duke was a bigger man and well, a duke and a mage. I knew vessels had pretty low social standing. Much like omegas did.

My throat tightened even more. Had I jumped to conclusions? I glanced at Hyde. For fuck's sake, I'd already told him. What the hell had I been thinking? I should have waited until I had a chance to talk to Eban. But Hyde had asked me a direct question and he was my employer.

My head started to pound. This was turning into a nightmare.

Chapter Six

The ride home in the car was tense. I sat in the front passenger seat next to the driver and had never hated privacy glass more. I felt like a traitor for leaving Eban alone in the back with his husband.

The need to know what was being said, what was being done, and if Eban was okay, was itching along my skin, making me squirm. The driver kept casting glances my way, but I was sure he could figure out what was going on. He'd been Hyde's driver for a while, he had to be used to the drama.

The car had barely parked before I flew out and opened the back door for Eban. He climbed out gracefully. Anxiously I ran my gaze all over him whilst my wolf whined. He looked unharmed but as Hyde got out of the car and stood beside him, I could taste the tension. Thick, weighted and apprehensive.

By some silent agreement, they walked into the house and straight to Eban's room. I followed behind them. Once in the bedroom, they still didn't speak. Eban just calmly took off his jacket and lay it on a chair. Then he started unbuttoning his shirt. That then joined the jacket. I glanced at Hyde, but he did not dismiss me. Surely he would if they were about to have sex?

Eban walked to his bedside table, opened the drawer and pulled out something on a thin gold chain. Whatever it was, it was wrapped in leather. He put it in his mouth and clenched it between his teeth. Then he lay face down on the bed. Moving his golden hair so that it spilled over the pillow and left his back bare.

Hyde started undoing his belt, and I started backing out of there. He glanced at me in surprise as if he had forgotten I was there. I nodded at him politely before fleeing. I hadn't gotten very far when the sound of the belt striking Eban assaulted my ears. I cowered and my wolf snarled, sending me images of its desire to rush back in there and tear Hyde's throat out.

The urge was so strong that it stopped me in my tracks and I stood there trembling impotently in the hallway. Unable to leave and refusing to go back in.

Mercifully the awful noises soon stopped and Hyde strode past me in the hall, without so much as a glance. I ran back into Eban's room. He hadn't moved. He was just lying there frozen on the bed. Five angry red lash marks across his back. One had broken the skin and a trickle of blood was seeping out. I stared in horror.

"Are you okay?" I gasped stupidly. His husband had just beaten him, of course he wasn't okay. A whimper escaped my throat as I realized the scars I had seen on his back weren't from kinky fun but from being ritually punished. Those scars had turned me on. Nausea heaved my stomach.

"How bad is it?" Eban asked tonelessly.

I stared at his back hopelessly. "If you were a shifter, you'd be healed in a couple of hours."

Eban sighed wearily. "Take a picture and show me."

Fumbling to get my phone out of my pocket I did as he bid. I stepped up close to the bed to show him the picture. He glanced at it for a moment before closing his eyes.

"There is a salve in the bedside cabinet. Can you apply it to the one that is bleeding please?"

Numbly I nodded and fetched the pot of cream. Horrified that this was such a regular occurrence that he kept supplies on hand to deal with the aftermath.

Awkwardly I perched on the bed and applied the ointment as gently as I could. Eban didn't even twitch or react in any way.

"I'm... I'm sorry," I breathed hoarsely.

Eban did suck in a breath then. "You were doing your job, it's fine."

I couldn't find the words. Nothing about the situation was fine. But it wasn't my culture and Eban was not mine. It was none of my business. Guilt gnawed at me relentlessly nevertheless.

The lash mark was nicely covered in the healing salve. I replaced the lid.

"Thank you. You may leave now," said Eban.

His dismissal felt like a punch in the gut even though it was no less than I deserved. I got to my feet, opened my mouth but no words would come.

I knew they were not married as most humans practiced marriage. Hyde was a mage and Eban was his vessel, more or less property. As any omega I claimed would be. But I would never treat an omega like this.

A small dark part of myself spoke up and asked how well I would take to my omega letting someone else fuck him in the toilets. I winced before rallying myself and asking how I would react if another alpha had cornered my omega and shoved him up against a wall. As I was growing increasingly convinced was the truth of what had happened.

A low growl escaped my throat to rumble darkly around the room. Eban recoiled on the bed and I felt a fresh wave of alarm and shame. The growl hadn't been directed at him for dismissing me. I opened my mouth again to try to explain, but then decided to run away instead before I dug myself an even deeper hole.

All but physically running, I left Eban alone. The door shut behind me, far too sharply and I winced yet again.

I escaped to my room, but it was not far enough away. It was only next door. I could still smell him, still feel his presence and his misery. And then, when he started softly sobbing, my shifter hearing could hear it perfectly. Groaning, I curled up in a ball on my bed and shoved the pillow over my ears. If only that worked to block out my thoughts as well.

Guilt and horror clawed at me. I needed to do something. I needed to earn Eban's forgiveness and help him. Even if it was the last thing I did.

Chapter Seven

The next day Eban was glib and cheery. Acting completely like his normal self. As much as I scrutinized his every movement, gesture and glance, I could not tell anything was wrong. He did not move stiffly. He did not seem scared or upset.

It made me wonder with a heavy, sinking feeling, just what other horrors he hid behind his charming yet bratty facade.

He pretty much ignored me completely, which irritated the hell out of me whilst also feeling completely deserved. The combination tied me up into disgruntled, grumpy knots.

Two days after the dinner party, Hyde left on business again. Aside from beating his husband, I'd not seen him spend any time with Eban. A fact I was increasingly grateful for. I had developed an utter dread of having to lie in my bed and listen to Hyde fucking Eban. I wasn't sure if my wolf would be able to cope. My wolf side had grown an unhealthy fixation on Eban. It probably was my alpha instincts wanting to protect him because he was vulnerable.

The evening of Hyde's departure, Eban announced he was going nightclubbing. I reread my briefing notes but there was nothing to indicate he was not allowed to. It seemed like a strange omission. A nightclub was a perfect place for Eban to get into all sorts of trouble and I desperately did not want him to get into trouble ever again. But

I was only a bodyguard. If he wanted to go nightclubbing, and his husband had put no restrictions on his movements, there was nothing I could do. Except tag along and try to stop any situations from arising.

So that evening, I found myself standing by the car waiting for him. The night time air was a little chilly. Summer was definitely surrendering to autumn. The sounds of the city washed over me, feeling a little oppressive. I really needed to let my wolf out and go on a run. Above the city lights and the clouds, the moon was full and I could feel her power. I was old enough to control it but I'd definitely be feeling extra horny tonight. Watching Eban gyrate on the dancefloor was going to be a test of my self restraint.

The front door of the house opened, and Eban emerged. His golden hair practically shimmering in the streetlights. The tightest white jeans I had ever seen, clung to his long shapely legs. A bright white crop top just about covered his nipples but left his toned midriff completely bare. A large white and gray fur coat flowed from his shoulders all the way down to his ankles.

Eban gracefully descended the stairs and stopped before me. He looked up at me with a puzzled expression and I flushed. I was standing there, staring like an idiot when I should be opening the car door for him. The knowledge did not unfreeze my muscles, and I'd never been so grateful for dark glasses in all my life. Hopefully, he couldn't tell I was all but drooling over him.

A look of alarm crossed his face. "It's fake! I'm not a monster!"

My mind scrambled to figure out what was going on. Luckily it was quick to decipher what Eban was talking about. Of course I knew the fur coat was fake. I could smell it from the moment he opened the front door. But it was a saving grace if he thought that was what my staring and incompetence was about.

"Glad to hear it," I said gruffly, and I finally opened the door.

He gave me a small relieved smile and got into the car. I carefully shut the door, walked to the front and took my own seat. My heart was fluttering crazily. Just because he had smiled at me. After everything I had done to him, It felt like a forgiveness that I did not deserve.

And then there was the look on his face as he had declared his coat was fake. He really did think humans wearing dead animals was monstrous. He wasn't merely concerned that it might offend me or think I would consider the mink or fox my relative. He wasn't as shallow as everyone thought he was. I wanted to get to know him. I wanted to have proper conversations. It was quite likely his mind was as dazzling as the rest of him.

I sighed heavily. No one had in-depth conversations with their bodyguard. We were never going to stay up all night talking and putting the world to rights. It was a foolish dream, so I resolutely put it from my mind.

When we arrived at the club, my heart sank. The queue was long and snaking. But Eban seemed undeterred. He flowed out of the car and started striding to the front door, ignoring the line and forcing me to scramble after him.

At the entrance, he leaned in close to the bouncer, said something I didn't catch, and was ushered in. I hurried after him.

A wall of sound crashed into me, nearly making me cower. It was loud, too loud for my shifter hearing I told myself. Absolutely nothing to do with my age. Luckily I had the foresight to be prepared, I fumbled in my pocket for the earplugs. I shoved them into my ears as Eban checked his coat into the cloakroom.

He turned to me with a grin, his gray eyes sparkling with excitement. The sight melted my heart and disintegrated my grumpy mood. Being here made Eban happy. It was worth a little discomfort on my part.

Eban practically bounced to the bar. He perched on a stool and ordered a ridiculous looking cocktail. There were already many pairs of eyes on him. I couldn't blame them, he was beautiful.

I stood beside him. He swiveled on the bar stool, sipped the straw of his drink and watched all the people with a gleam in his eyes. The club was busy but not full yet. It was a very gay crowd that milled around and there were some very pleasing outfits to admire. There were only a few people on the dancefloor and none of them could dance very well but they were obviously having fun.

"Stop cockblocking me!" hissed Eban, startling me from my thoughts.

I looked around. Several people were clearly eyeing him up, but no one was approaching him. Our end of the bar was empty. Like a little bubble of calm.

I glanced down at him. "It's literally my job."

He sighed and looked up at me with a pleading look. "Oh darling, just let people talk to me, buy my drinks. A bit of harmless flirting. Please?"

It was probably a terrible idea, but I understood his longing. Here he wasn't Lord du Fray, Hyde's husband or a vessel. He was simply a gorgeous young man.

Huffing my reluctance I moved down the bar away from him to take up a seat around five places down. I ordered a whiskey and pretended to be broodingly drinking on my own. But my full attention was fully fixed on Eban. Seconds later they swooped and he was surrounded by admirers. A big guy bought him a drink and took up the seat next to him. Eban beamed at him and chatted away happily.

I took a big sip of my whiskey and thought of ordering another. It was not surprising that Eban was lonely. He lived in a castle sized house with just his asshole husband who was often away. Everyone else was staff. Including me. People who worked for you were not your friends. At the dinner party, conversations had been laced with double meanings, thinly veiled insults. I couldn't imagine he enjoyed being amongst that nest of vipers. Never mind whatever had happened in the bathroom and then the repercussions of my snitching.

I drowned my drink. Eban deserved company, conversation, connection. It was stupid to yearn to swap places with the big guy. To long to be the one sitting next to him and making him laugh. I was just his bodyguard. His rude grumpy bodyguard who had called him ugly and gotten him beaten by his husband. I ordered another drink. He was never going to like me.

The memory of when we had first met played in my mind. The sound of his musical laughter echoed in my ears. "I think I'm going to like you," he had said. His eyes had sparkled. And then I had gone and ruined it all. I looked down at my new drink, it was empty. I had already downed it.

"Hi!" said a voice by my side.

I turned my head to find a very cute human with dark curls and sky blue eyes. His leather shorts left nothing to the imagination and his black mesh top failed to hide his pierced nipples.

"Sorry, I'm not in the mood for company," I said.

The twink gave me a long lingering look, up and down my whole body. My cock twitched.

"Shame," he said with a mischievous glint in his eyes. "Come and find me if you decide you want to forget all about him."

He winked and melted back into the crowd. I blinked. Was I really that readable? I supposed drinking alone in a nightclub was a clear indication of a broken heart. Except my heart wasn't broken. I just had developed a bit of a crush, that was all. I'd get over it.

If I wasn't working, I'd go after the hot twink, I told myself. But I knew that wasn't true. My stupid wolf had fixated on Eban and wanted no one else. I sighed. I'd just have to pine for a while before my wolf got the idea that it was never going to happen. Then I'd be able to get on with my life.

I looked over at Eban, but the end of the bar was empty. Growling, I stormed over to the dancefloor and sure enough he was there. My feet took root and I was frozen to the spot as I stared at him. I had known he could dance. It was obvious in the grace with which he moved. But actually seeing it was short circuiting my mind. He flowed in perfect time to the music. The muscles of his naked, bare midriff undulating. The big guy who he had been talking to was grinding behind him, then his hands grabbed Eban's hips. I was there in a flash, snarling up at the human.

"I wouldn't if I were you. His husband is a very dangerous man."

The human's eyes widened and he jumped back. Nobody else could have heard what I had said but they all saw the big guy's reaction and they all followed his lead until Eban was standing alone in his own little island in the middle of the dancefloor. Eban looked around at the crowd, glared at me and stormed off.

I hurried after him. He passed the cloakroom without stopping and all but ran up the stairs to the street. I ran after him.

"Your coat!" I reminded him.

He didn't look back or slow his pace. He merely gave me a dismissive gesture with his hand. I jogged up to him, pulling the earplugs out of my ears as I went.

"I'll call the driver," I said, as I reached for my phone.

"I want to walk," snapped Eban.

I glanced around. It wasn't an awful part of the city but it was getting late and something about Eban just screamed money. He was very obviously a rich kid. Muggers would be drawn like flies to honey.

"I'm not sure that's safe," I tried.

He ignored me and just continued to stride along.

"I'm sorry," I said. "But you can't dry hump men on the dancefloor, Hyde..."

There was no point finishing that sentence. Eban knew full well what he was and was not permitted to do. Why he had no self preservation was beyond me.

"I just wanted to have some fun," he said and there was a faint slurring to his words. He was drunk. He must have started drinking earlier, at home. Alone in his room.

"Do you know what fun is, Bastion?" he demanded, but I could not answer him because a thousand butterflies had taken flight in my stomach at the sound of him saying my name.

"Do you know how to feel alive?" he continued.

He put one hand on a lamppost and twirled around it. Like it was a pole in a strip club. Then he bounded away from it. We were approaching a bridge. I sent a text to the driver with our location while Eban danced drunkenly around the street with far more grace than was fair.

Suddenly, he jumped up onto the wall of the bridge.

"Do you know how to live a little!" he declared with his arms outstretched.

I ran up to him, heart hammering in my chest. He was too drunk and in too strange a mood to be standing on the edge of a bridge.

"Get down!" I snapped but I wasn't going to wait for him to obey. I grabbed his waist and pulled him down to stand next to me.

He blinked up at me. My hands were around his waist. Half on his jeans, half on the bare skin of his exposed midriff. We were standing toe to toe. My mind was shrieking in delight about the few seconds I had held him in the air. His slight weight in my arms had been electric.

Now he was close enough to feel his body heat. His delicious scent was pouring into every pore of my body. He swayed slightly and I held him steady, breathing him in. His eyes were fixed on mine but I couldn't read his expression. His pupils were wide and his breaths were shallow and fast.

The car pulled up behind us and I was both dismayed and relieved. I bundled Eban into the back seat before I did something crazy like kiss him. I knew the way he had looked at me would haunt me forever. He had looked at me as if he liked me, as if he wanted me.

I huffed out a shaky breath. I was being ridiculous. There was no way Lord Eban du Fray fancied me.

Chapter Eight

I pounded on the treadmill until sweat dripped into my eyes. Still, I did not stop. I was trying to run all my stupid spiraling thoughts out of my head. But they were being stubborn and refusing to move, at this rate I'd be running forever.

The gym in Eban's home was lovely and well equipped. I considered moving to the rowing machine. I needed to get the way Eban had looked at me last night out of my mind.

A movement in the doorway caught my eye. It was Eban, he looked a little disheveled and flushed. I hit the stop button on the treadmill, grabbed my towel to wipe the sweat out of my eyes and turned to face him.

He stood motionless in the doorway. His gaze tracking down my sweaty body. My black tee shirt was tight and my gray sweatpants left little to the imagination. I hadn't expected to see anyone.

Eban took a deep breath, licked his lips and dragged his gaze up to my eyes.

"Umm... can you call Hyde?"

I blinked in confusion for a moment before remembering that Eban did not have a phone. He wasn't allowed to have one. Was he not even permitted to use a landline to call his own husband? My inner wolf snarled in anger but I ignored it. Eban did not want my pity.

"Sure," I said, stepping off the treadmill and reaching for my sweatshirt. My phone was in the pocket. "What's the message?"

Eban flushed and looked away. "I'm ripe."

Oh. Ripe. That meant he was full of magic and needed to be emptied. And that meant he needed sex. I wondered if it was like being in heat. Were lust and desire rolling through his body uncontrollably? Was he desperate to be touched, to be filled?

I swallowed dryly and turned slightly away from him. Damn gray sweatpants. I didn't want him to see my arousal.

"Ripe is a disgusting word for it," I muttered inanely, scrambling for something to say.

Eban chuckled. "Oh darling, it really is a vile term. I loathe it."

I smiled at him with the phone pressed to my ear. It felt strange to be binding over such a topic but it thrilled me that we were.

Hyde answered on the third ring. "Hello, it's Bastion here. Eban is ripe." I knew I was supposed to drop a 'my lord,' in there somewhere but I couldn't bring myself to do it. Hyde had never called me up on it before.

He swore. "I'm in China, I can't get back. You will have to do it."

"P...pardon?"

"It's one of the reasons I hired you, your innate shifter magic is enough to call his magic out and empty him."

I opened my mouth several times before any words came out. "That wasn't in the job description."

"Consider it a perk," he said dryly.

"You seriously want me to fuck your husband?"

"Yes," he snapped and the line went dead.

Numbly, I turned back to Eban. He had gone as white as a sheet and his eyes were huge.

"Umm... he is in China and he told me to do it," I said needlessly. My end of the conversation had made it clear enough.

Eban nodded abruptly. "Come to my room in an hour," he said and then he was gone.

I stared at the empty doorway for far too long. Unable to comprehend the turn of events. Was I really going to get to sleep with Eban? Was this really happening?

I slapped myself in the face, hard. "Ow!" I exclaimed out loud. Okay, so I wasn't dreaming. I really was about to have Eban in my arms, with his husband's permission.

An hour later I stood outside Eban's door and hesitated. All sorts of erotic images playing in my mind. Kissing Eban. Eban writhing and moaning beneath me, no, as he rode me. He seemed the type. He'd look at me with that naughty twinkle in his eye and I'd be helpless before him. He always moved so gracefully, so seductively. I just knew he would be a passionate, confident lover. Eager to give and receive pleasure and not shy to demand what he wanted.

He flirted constantly, with nearly everyone. It was a sure sign he had a high sex drive and right now he was ripe, which as far as I could tell was like an omega being in heat. The way he had looked at me last night and even earlier, in the gym. He wanted me. He needed me and I was going to serve him well.

I knocked sharply, my hands shaking in anticipation. A muffled answer that sounded like "Come in," had me bounding through the door.

Eban was sitting on the edge of his bed. His head bowed and his gaze fixed on his hands in his lap. He was wearing a long white nightgown.

My excitement withered and died. Nothing about his body language spoke of desire or need. The atmosphere in the room was stifling. Tense and somber.

He didn't want me. I must have misread the look in his eye. Or maybe he liked to look but when it came to actually having sex with a shifter, he recoiled in disgust.

"I... I can find someone else. Someone on the staff must have magic," I offered weakly.

"No!" he said sharply and shook his head. But before hope could tentatively flicker to life within me, he spoke again. "There isn't anyone with magic and Hyde told you to do it. I don't want to get into trouble."

A long silence stretched. I could hear the city traffic. I did not want to take him if he didn't want me. But he needed to be emptied. And I really didn't want him to get into trouble.

"Okay," I whispered.

He nodded decisively and got onto the bed. There was something on a gold chain around his neck and with cold horror I recognized it as the leather he had bitten down on when being lashed by Hyde.

Eban lay back on the pillows, clenched the leather between his teeth, spread his legs and scrunched his eyes up tight. I stared in dismay. He was acting as if I was about to beat him. Did he really think having sex with me was as bad as being whipped by Hyde?

I stepped closer, to talk to him. To say something reassuring, but as I did so, his hands twisted in the sheets, clutching them, bracing himself.

The sight broke my heart and stole all of my words. I could not do this. I opened my mouth to say so but then the scent of his arousal washed over me. It was strong and had a strange taste to it. It was potent and urgent and not too dissimilar from a heat.

A flurry of thoughts hit me. Vessels could die if they were not emptied. Eban had said there was no one else who could do it. Omegas sometimes became overwhelmed by their heats and were scared. Eban was like an omega, he needed someone to help him through this. He needed help to let go and surrender to his body's needs.

I took a deep breath and took off my clothes. I had showered and changed into a clean tee shirt and gray sweatpants because Eban had seemed to appreciate them, but he hadn't even looked at me.

As soon as I was naked, I climbed onto the bed and kneeled between his spread legs. He didn't move. Just breathed in short rapid breaths.

I stared at him awkwardly. Kissing was normally a good way to start, but judging by the way he clenched the leather bound thing between his teeth, I got the distinct impression that it was off the menu. I also got the distinct impression he was desperate for me to get on with it.

Swallowing over the lump in my throat, I gently pushed his nightgown up and over his hips. His cock was full and tantalizing. But I didn't think he would let me suck it.

Another thought suddenly struck me. Eban was human. Humans did not get slick.

"Umm... do you need lube?" I asked awkwardly.

He moved a hand up to his mouth and removed the leather. "I've done it," he said and bit down on the thing again.

I stared down at his motionless, rigid body. My cock throbbed, it had no morals. I was an alpha and the moon had been full yesterday. Sex was on offer and that was all my cock needed to know.

But I wasn't my cock. I couldn't just shove it in and be happy.

"Can I give you a blowjob?" I asked.

His eyes flew open to stare at me. I'd never seen anyone look more incredulous or shocked. I stared back calmly even though my heart was breaking. He clearly believed all the nonsense people spouted about shifters and alphas. But we weren't all aggressive and dominating in bed and yes some big bad alpha shifters liked to suck cock.

I let him see how serious I was, how much I really wanted to. After a long, long moment, he gave a tiny nod. Grinning in delight, I lowered myself down into position, my mouth already watering at the thought of what I was about to taste.

His cock was beautiful. A good length and girth for his size. Pale. like the rest of him but flushed pink at the head. I ran my tongue from his balls all the way up to his tip, coating the underneath of his cock with my saliva.

He keened around the thing in his mouth, and his hips rose up off the bed. I chuckled and placed one hand on his firm abdomen to hold him down, then I set to work worshiping his cock. Trailing my tongue over every bit of him. Exploring every crevice and ridge whilst he whimpered.

Then I slipped my mouth over his cockhead and the sounds of his muffled cries were music to my ears. I took him in deeper, all the way to the back of my throat. I hollowed out my cheeks, and he came with a strangled moan. I swallowed him down eagerly, feeling like any minute I was going to blow my own load. That had been super quick. I must have done a very good job.

When I was sure he was spent, I released him with a wet plop and looked up with a pleased grin. His eyes were still closed and his hands were still clutching the sheets but his face was all flushed and even more beautiful than usual. He was breathing heavily, almost panting.

"Was that the best blowjob you have ever had?" I asked smugly. I knew I was good.

He spat the thing in his mouth out. "That was the onl..." he trailed off and shuddered. "Yes," he finished weakly.

I was grinning so widely my face hurt. I'd never been so proud of anything in all my life. Giving Eban pleasure was my new favorite thing to do.

"I need... I need," he stammered breathlessly.

"I know, babe, I know."

He was still full of magic and all the best blowjobs in the world would not solve that. Carefully, I positioned myself over him. Desire and lust pounding through me. I needed him. Wanted him more than anything. Feverishly, I started pushing into him. He winced.

"You're huge!" he gasped.

What had he been expecting? I was an alpha wolf shifter. I pushed some more, and he whimpered but not a good whimper. I froze. Then moved back to kneeling between his legs.

"Can I use my fingers?" I asked.

He nodded.

Gently, I spread his legs further apart. Then I teased a finger around his hole. There was a lot of lube. I slipped my finger inside easily. He had opened himself up well. I added a second finger, and he groaned before scrambling to shove the leather back in his mouth. I was beginning to hate that thing. But he seemed to need it.

Slowly, I worked my fingers in and out and side to side. Aiming to pleasure him as well as to open him up even more. I found his prostate and stroked it gently. His moans became more fervent and his legs spread even wider as all his muscles relaxed. It was working.

I was managing to calm him down and get him properly in the mood. His body's need for his magic to be emptied had clearly not got his mind and soul on board. I did not know for sure if it was being ripe that had been unsettling him or if it was simply he did not want to have sex with a shifter. Either way, I was determined to give him so much pleasure that his arousal made him forget everything.

It looked like I was nearly there. I added a third finger and he gasped. A good, lust-filled gasp. I grinned. The heat of his hot tight flesh around my fingers was divine, I couldn't wait to sink my cock into him.

My three fingers were sliding in and out of him easily. He was as ready as he was going to be. I looked up at his face. His eyes were still tightly closed but his head was tilted up and there was a slackness in his jaw that spoke of pleasure.

I rolled him over onto his front, he went bonelessly with no objection. I stayed kneeling and pulled his hips up onto my lap, leaving his shoulders and head firmly on the mattress.

"Ready to try again?" I asked.

A garbled murmur that sounded positive was my answer. Trembling with anticipation, I lined my cock up to his hole. Tentatively I started to push in. The tip of my swollen cockhead eased into his tight heat. A deep hungry groan escaped my chest. He felt divine. I pushed in some more. He was making strangled, gasping noises but they sounded like happy ones, so I kept going. Kept filling him, stretching him, taking him.

'Mine,' declared my wolf happily. I groaned as I slid in the last inch. My fingers digging into his hips. I was balls deep in Eban and it was incredible.

Fighting my hips to stay still, I gave him time to adjust.

"Are you okay, babe?" I gasped.

Another incomprehensible murmur but his head moved against the pillow in an approximation of a nod. So I started to move. Tortuously slowly at first until I was certain he was comfortable and had stretched around my large size. He started moaning beautifully and giving happy whimpers, so I let my hips take over and pick up the fast pace they were desperate for.

I held him tightly and pummeled into him, he started coming, clenching tightly around my cock, spasming and screaming his pleasure. It was incredible. I groaned as my knot started to form. Swearing profusely I pulled out a little. Eban was not an omega, a knot would be too much for him and likely hurt him. I thrust with just the top part of my cock until with a growl of satisfaction my orgasm overtook me.

A wave of dizziness washed over me, followed by a strange tingling sensation all along my skin, all along my insides. His magic, I realized with surprise. I had not expected to feel it so viscerally.

I collapsed beside him with a spent groan and pulled him into a spoon. The feel of him all warm in my arms was everything I wanted. I sighed happily.

"What are you doing?" he asked sharply.

I blinked in confusion. "Um, snuggling?"

"Well don't!" he snapped. "You may leave now."

I sat up, but he kept his back to me. I couldn't see his face. His words felt like a punch in the gut.

"Damn, Eban. We just had sex, no need to be so cold."

"So? We are not lovers. That was merely functional."

I placed my hand on his shoulder to try to turn him over to face me but he tensed up every muscle in his body against me.

"I... I didn't mean it to be functional," I stammered hopelessly. Feeling like I was lost on a stormy sea without a compass. I had no idea what to say or do.

"Get out!" he snarled at me.

I scrambled out of bed, intending to walk around it and face him.

"Eban, I'm sorry. Did I hurt you?"

I was by the foot of the bed. He sat up and finally faced me, clutching the sheet to his chest. His eyes were blazing with anger and there were tears on his cheeks.

"You've followed your orders, even though it wasn't in your job description! Now get out"

The snide words I had said to Hyde flashed before me. Eban had been standing right there. I hadn't thought about how it might sound. Cold horror doused me like a bucket of water. From Eban's perspective, it would have sounded awful. Like I didn't want to sleep with him. Like I was only doing it begrudgingly to keep my job.

I stared at Eban helplessly. "I... I."

"Get out!" he yelled and the bedside lamp flew past my head to smash on the floor.

I flinched, and like a coward I grabbed my clothes and fled.

Chapter Nine

I avoided Eban the next day. It may have been cowardly but I told myself that it was what he wanted.

My plan was to silently stalk him by staying in the next room, making sure I was always within earshot so I could still do my job. Thankfully, he didn't have any plans to go out.

I smelled the alcohol at breakfast, and he didn't emerge from his rooms. It made my life easier as I just needed to stay lurking in mine. Though, there probably wasn't much of a threat of anything happening in the safety of his home. Hyde had been confident that he had weeded out anyone on his staff who might be foolish enough to sleep with Eban.

However, I was starting to wonder just how much a problem that really was. Hyde had talked about Eban as if he was insatiable and Eban was certainly a flirt who seemed to thrive on attention. But images from the night before crowded my mind. Eban hadn't seemed into it at all. He had acted like sex was an ordeal he needed to get through. Maybe I was big-headed, but no one had ever accused me of being a terrible lover. Surely, it couldn't have been because I was so unsatisfactory?

Was it really because he was so insulted by the thought I didn't want him, and was just reluctantly following orders? Was it because I was a shifter and the thought of having to sleep with me was demeaning? Was he upset that his husband hadn't come home for him?

I groaned and buried my head in my hands. So many questions that I'd likely never have any answers for. Eban was upset with me, for whatever reason and that knowledge hurt. More so because I had no idea how to fix it. With that thought my mind turned once again to trying to puzzle out the source of his displeasure. If I could figure out why, then I could work out how to make amends.

My wolf was whining and dejected. Demanded that I go hunt some rabbits or a deer and lay my kill at his feet as an offering. A courting gift. Angrily I ignored the urge. It was old-fashioned even for shifters. Eban was human, I was quite sure he wouldn't be impressed at being presented with dead prey. The way to make him happy was to puzzle out what had gone wrong and then do something about it.

Maybe it was simply that he didn't like sex. Maybe he was scared of it, carried too much trauma to enjoy it. I knew his husband had married him on his eighteenth birthday. That was very young for a human. Had Eban been hurt and misused for ten long years? Was his flirtatious charm just a facade? Nothing more than bravado? Armor. Was the real Eban the one I had been in bed with last night? Scared. Reluctant. Clutching the sheets in dread. Demanding to be alone afterwards with tears on his face because it had been a terrible ordeal.

My stomach heaved and I thought I was going to be sick. That couldn't be it. I could not be last in a long line of men to abuse him. My mind tried to scrabble away from that thought in horror. Or possibly denial.

I took out my phone and started Googling. At first I had no idea what to search for but then I slowly found my way. It felt like a solid lump of ice formed in my gut as I read on. Acting very sexually was a form of hypersexuality and that was a known trauma response.

It didn't mean I was right though. I wasn't a doctor, I couldn't diagnose anyone. Eban could be fine. My ego could just be refusing to accept that he simply did not like me. But my mind helpfully supplied images. The way the duke had him pressed against the wall. The way his husband treated him and talked about him. The sounds of his nightmare. The look of surprise on Eban's face in the changing room when we had been alone but I hadn't done anything.

A loud crash in the hallway had me jumping to my feet. I ran out. Eban was sprawled on his front on the floor, a side table and all its contents beside him. The smell of alcohol invaded my nose but I could not smell any blood or injuries. He was unhurt.

"How drunk are you?" I asked.

"Very and not enough," he answered.

He flopped over onto his back and peered at me with blurry eyes.

"Why are you everywhere I look? All hulking and handsome?"

My wolf wanted to wag its tail at being called handsome. I sternly ignored it.

"I'm your bodyguard, I'm supposed to be everywhere you are."

He made a displeased noise and continued to stare at me. I gazed back into his beautiful gray eyes and something changed. Maybe it was because he was very drunk, or maybe it was because of everything I had just been reading, but suddenly he didn't look snide, bratty and annoying. I looked into his eyes and saw nothing but sadness, loneliness and fear.

He looked haunted and hunted, and I longed to throw my arms around him and make everything alright.

But suddenly he was moving, hauling himself to his feet and staggering off down the hall. I chased after him.

"Where are you going?" I asked.

"Swimming."

I looked at the state of him. "You'll drown."

He laughed. "I should be so lucky."

As his words sunk into my soul, branding it forever, he continued on his way. He couldn't mean that. He was just being flippant, surely?

He fumbled with the door handle for a moment and my tension eased a little. He was far too drunk to make it up the stairs and to the pool. I wasn't going to have to stop him and get into an argument.

The door opened and he wobbled up the steep flight of stairs. I followed closely behind him, convinced any moment he was going to tumble backwards into my arms. But somehow he made it to the top and made a beeline for the pool.

I stalked after him. He clumsily yanked his tee shirt over his head, getting stuck for a few moments. My breath sucked in at the sight of his naked chest. He really was so very beautiful.

He teetered to the edge of the pool.

"Eban, no! You are too drunk," I said sternly, putting all my alpha authority into my voice. He needed to listen.

He glared at me in clear indignation and poked me in the chest. "You don't get to tell me what to do!"

"Yes, I do."

His eyes narrowed. "Why? Because you are all brooding and gorgeous and kind in bed?"

I stared at him. Kind? I didn't think I had been kind. I'd been far too horny, far too stupid to be truly kind. I hadn't figured it out then and had mostly thought he was acting strange because it was an effect of being ripe. If he thought that last night had been kind, what on earth was he used to?

Whatever he saw in my expression, he clearly didn't like. He huffed in annoyance and stepped back away from me before losing his balance and falling into the pool with an almighty splash.

THE BODYGUARD'S VESSEL

The pool probably wasn't deep. It was likely he could stand up in it. Or that the shock would sober him up, and if not, he was such a graceful little shit, he probably could swim whilst stupidly drunk.

I didn't wait to find out. I dived in after him, fully clothed. I found him quickly under the water and pulled him into my arms. The pool was shallow enough for me to stand up in, holding him in a bridal carry. I stared down at him. Under the water he had flung his arms around my neck. He didn't remove them. Just stared up at me as water streamed off of him.

I reflexively tightened my grip on him. My wolf never wanted to let him go. 'Mine,' it insisted. Except he wasn't mine. He was Hyde's and that was never going to change.

The pool was heated but the air was chilly.

"Let's get you inside and dried off before you catch a cold," I said, when there were so many other things I wanted to say.

He stared deep into my eyes. An intense look in his gaze as if he wanted to say things too. I waited with bated breath, but after a long tense moment he merely sighed and rested his head against my shoulder. That small, trusting gesture, made my heart go crazy.

I carried him out of the pool and down the stairs. All the way to his room. I only wished I could keep on walking and carry him out of the house and away from his life.

But he wasn't mine and I could not keep him.

Chapter Ten

Two days later Hyde came home. I stood on the steps of the house with the other key staff to greet him. He nodded at the butler and some of the others before his eyes met mine. I nodded a greeting apprehensively. I'd slept with the man's husband. By his permission, but it was still uncomfortable.

"Has he been behaving?" he asked.

"Yes, my lord," I managed.

He nodded and strode past me. Seemingly content with that. I let out a breath I hadn't realized I had been holding. Hyde clearly didn't have a problem with me at all. It meant that either he did not care for Eban in the slightest, or he was polyamorously minded. Somehow, I thought the former was far more likely. Still, I was surprised he didn't seem to have a shred of possessiveness in him. No trace of irrational jealousy. But he wasn't an alpha werewolf. I couldn't judge people by the way I ticked.

If Eban was mine, I'd rip the eyes out of anyone who so much as looked at him funny. But he was not mine and never would be.

I stepped back into the house and went to check on Eban. I may have figured out why sleeping with me had made him so upset but I didn't have a clue what to do about it. The best I could do was be attentive.

I found him in his rooms, at the breakfast table eating toast while wearing an emerald green dressing gown. Looking none the worse for wear for getting outrageously drunk again the day before.

"Not welcoming your husband home?" I commented.

He shrugged eloquently. "He knows where I am."

I took a seat opposite him, feeling strangely proud of Eban. He didn't fawn over or cower before his powerful asshole of a husband. Given just how much power Hyde had over him, it was no small feat.

Hyde was a heavyset man in his mid-forties. Eban was lithe and slender and half his age. Hyde was stronger in all ways. He had the advantage of physical strength, age and wealth. He was also a mage whilst Eban was merely a vessel. Everything was stacked against Eban. But he still didn't just roll over and bare his throat. I admired that about him.

I closed my eyes and took a steadying breath. Pining helped no one. It was time to focus on my job.

"Are you going shopping today?" I asked.

Eban raised one eyebrow and gave me a quizzical look. "No. Why?"

"I thought you might want something new to wear for the party."

He gave me a strange look. "What party?"

My fingers itched to go to my room, pick up my tablet and check but I knew I hadn't imagined it.

"It's in the calendar, you are hosting a party here tonight."

Eban threw his toast down. "It definitely says party? Not dinner party or soiree?"

I nodded, too confused by his reaction to say anything. He was a social butterfly, surely he loved parties? Was he pissed off that Hyde hadn't bothered to tell him?

Eban abruptly got to his feet, the chair crashing backwards behind him. He whirled and flew into his bedroom, slamming the door behind him.

I stared at the shut door for a long moment, longing to go talk to him. I wanted to find out what was wrong and fix it or if that was not possible, comfort him.

I got to my feet and forced myself to walk away. I was just his bodyguard. There was plenty to do to prepare for guests this evening. My job was to keep him safe and out of trouble, nothing more.

The fifty or so guests assembled in the largest drawing room. The fire crackled merrily in the large marble fireplace. One of Hyde's footmen softly played the grand piano that was tucked in the corner. Other staff swanned around with silver trays of drinks.

The guests stood around in small groups or sat together on the settees and chaise lounges that were dotted around. It did not look terrible to me. I stood with my back against the wall, just by the door. Hands clasped in front of me and eyes fixed on Eban like a hawk. It was my job after all.

He moved through the crowd effortlessly. He smiled and laughed and seemed utterly at ease. In his element. I caught several men and some women staring at him with avarice glinting in their eyes. I was sure he was enjoying the attention.

But his reaction to learning about the party haunted me and kept me on edge. Hopefully, he was just pissed off that Hyde hadn't bothered to tell him. Even so, I knew I would not relax until the last guest had gone home.

Eban knocked back another drink. That man drank far too much. I suspected he also partook in other substances that were no good for him, but so far he had kept that out of my sight.

The sound of his laughter reached me, and my wolf whined. It wanted to go up to him and bask in his presence. I ignored it. Watching him from afar was as good as it was going to get.

He looked incredible, as always. He was wearing one of the gray outfits he had bought on the shopping trip. It was like a long loose silky shirt that cinched at his narrow waist before falling to his mid-thigh. His trousers were a darker gray and smooth and tight. Perfect for showing off his long shapely legs. His golden hair shone like a halo, making him stand out vividly in the crowd. He was by far the most stunning person there.

The man he was talking to placed his hand on his elbow. Something about the gesture was so acquisitive. 'Mine!' growled my wolf. Just because you have had him once, doesn't mean he is yours. I reminded myself. 'Mine!' insisted my wolf stubbornly.

The man did not release Eban. Instead, he steered him to a nearby chaise lounge and sat Eban down. Another man sat on the other side of Eban, far too close. I frowned.

Hyde rang a tiny silver hand bell. The sound ringing out clearly over the hum of conversation and the background tinkling of the piano. Several delighted cheers rose up. I stared at Hyde in confusion, what the hell was going on?

He grinned, turned back to the woman he had been talking to, ripped her blouse open and buried his head in her breasts. The room erupted into a flurry of movement as clothes were similarly divested.

I looked around in shock. An orgy? I had not been expecting that. My gaze flew to Eban, the men sitting with him had their hands all over him. Eban's eyes were closed. I took a step towards him without thinking.

I glanced at Hyde, he was sitting opposite his husband, ten feet away at the most. He had to know. Of course he knew, I told myself angrily. He had brought Eban to an orgy.

My attention snapped back to Eban. Was he having fun? Should I intervene or was it none of my business? Was this what he had been upset about?

I hopped from foot to foot in indecision. Staff bustled about lighting the incense burners I'd been curious about earlier. Thick billowing smoke poured out of them. Far more than I had expected. The smell reached me. Tangent, potent, sickly. An aphrodisiac? A relaxant? Both?

I snatched my handkerchief out of my pocket and hurriedly made an impromptu mask. Fuck Hyde. He should have told me about this. He didn't get to drug me just because I was his employee.

Luckily I was outside the circle of braziers, and the smoke was billowing inwards, over the guest. Either clever ventilation or a decadent use of magic. Impatiently I waited for the smoke to clear so I could see Eban.

As soon as it did, I saw he had slid down onto the floor by the chaise lounge. The men had slid down with him and undone the buttons of his silky top and his shoulder was bare. He was leaning heavily into the lap of one guy while the other was working his tight trousers down. I sucked in a breath and stepped closer. Eban's eyes were closed. He winced, and suddenly I was striding forward.

Two men were humping on the floor while a young redhead guy watched them whilst stroking himself. I grabbed him by the scruff of his neck, dragging him with me. He gave a little yelp of surprise but didn't struggle.

I loomed over Eban and the men undressing him. I reached down with one hand and pulled him to his feet as I shoved the redhead down in his place. The trio blinked at each other in surprise, cast me a brief puzzled glance, but then grinned at each other and started fondling one another.

I watched for a brief second to make sure the redhead was happy. Satisfied that he was, I strode away, hauling Eban with me.

We made it out of the drawing room, to the silent and empty hallway outside. Eban was not managing to get his feet under him, so I pushed him against the wall and held him there, steadying him.

"Are you okay?" I asked.

He raised his beautiful eyes to mine. His pupils were blown, his gaze all unfocused and hazy. He was completely out of it. I wasn't sure if he could even see me. I yanked my homemade mask off in case it was confusing him, but it didn't seem to make a difference.

I ran my gaze all over his body, checking for injuries. His hair was all tousled and messy. His undone clothes hung loosely, baring one shoulder and one nipple. His trousers were bunched around his knees.

But he did not look physically harmed. I tried to pull his trousers up for him, while he swayed against the wall but they were too tight to be cooperative.

He stared up at me blearily but intently. I stared back and swallowed tightly. A loud thump from inside the drawing room made me jump. I needed to get him away from here before his husband realized he was missing. Hyde had made him come, so no doubt wanted him there.

I scooped Eban up into my arms and carried him to his rooms. I gently placed him on his bed and my wolf refused to let him go. After a long moment of arguing with myself, I managed to move far away enough to undress him. Then I found some soft pajamas and manhandled him into them. He was all warm and pliant beneath my touch. Soft, helpless, vulnerable.

The thought of him in that orgy sickened my soul and filled me with rage. He seemed far more out of it than the guests had been. Had Hyde put something in his drink? I wouldn't put it past him.

I pulled up a chair and sat beside Eban's bed. I couldn't bear to leave him alone while he was still awake. He was blinking blankly at the canopy above his head. Out of it but still conscious.

I held his hand and waited for him to fall asleep. I would wait all night if I needed to.

Sitting there, holding his hand whilst listening to his soft breathing was strangely relaxing. 'Mine,' breathed my wolf happily. Not yours, I told it sternly.

After a while Eban turned his head to look at me. Confusion clear in his still unfocused eyes.

"Where...?" he whispered so faintly I only just heard him.

"Safe," I said. "In your room."

He blinked at me slowly. "Take me back. Entertain guests. Hyde."

I clenched his hand tighter, putting my other hand over his too. He was not fucking entertainment for Hyde's guests. Not while I was alive.

"No," I said simply.

Eban stared back at me. A look of fear started to cross his face.

"I'll deal with Hyde. I'll tell him it's my fault. I'll take care of it. Trust me."

Eban stared at me. The fear faded and his expression softened. I smiled at him. He smiled back. A big, bright, happy smile that was dazzling to see. Then his eyes fluttered closed and he fell asleep.

I watched him sleeping as my heart thudded in my chest and a thousand butterflies swarmed in my gut.

I shuffled my chair closer and stayed the night.

Chapter Eleven

Hyde burst in with the dawn light. Eban scrambled to a sitting position, snatching his hand back from mine. Hyde's anger filled the room like a dark cloud.

"Why did you think you could slope off last night! Sweetening up my guests is one of the few things you are good for!"

I jumped to my feet and stepped in front of Hyde. I was bigger than him and taller. He looked up at me in clear astonishment that I would get in his way.

"The fault is mine, my lord. I took my instructions to stop Lord du Fray from sleeping around too literally. I should have realized that your parties were an exception."

Hyde glared up at me.

"Do you think I'm stupid?" he snapped. "Did you fuck him?"

Now he was jealous? Or was he simply annoyed that I would presume to pull Eban out of the orgy to have him for myself?

I narrowed my eyes and crossed my arms. "Not last night."

Behind me, Eban flinched. A wave of guilt washed over me. That hadn't been very tactful of me. But I wanted to remind Hyde that he did not have the moral high ground. He had previously all but ordered me to sleep with his husband.

Hyde did not rise to the bait. Instead, he side-stepped around me and strode up to Eban. I thought for a moment he was going to strike Eban and my wolf urged me to act, but Hyde merely placed a hand on the crown of Eban's Head. It looked harmless, but Eban cowered and closed his eyes.

I winced. I should have stopped Hyde. I had promised Eban that I would deal with everything and that it was going to be okay. Somehow I needed to protect him, but without crossing the line that would get me fired. If I was thrown out on my ear, I'd never be able to help Eban ever again.

My wolf disagreed with me. It was very confident that it could just rip out Hyde's throat and solve the problem that way. It was a struggle to ignore it.

"I'm sorry," I said again, desperate to draw attention to myself. "I should have asked you, but you seemed occupied."

Hyde glared at me again, pulling his hand back from Eban's head. It had worked, he was focusing his anger on me, not his husband.

"See it does not happen again," he snapped and stormed out of the door.

I was by Eban's side in an instant. Kneeling by his bedside. Anxiously running my gaze all over him. I yearned to take his hand again but I had the distinct feeling he wasn't going to let me.

"Are you okay? What did he do to you?" I babbled.

"Checked my memories," answered Eban softly.

My mouth fell open. "He read your mind?"

Eban gave a tiny nod. Judging by his reaction and his pale expression, it was far from a pleasant experience. However, all things considered, I thought we had mostly got away with it.

Suddenly, Eban's gray eyes were fixed on me. Intense and furious. My heart sank. It didn't seem like Eban shared my opinion. He looked livid. A horrible thought struck me. Hyde had checked his memories, but that didn't mean Eban had access to them. He had been completely out of it, and Hyde had not explicitly said that he was happy with what he had seen.

"Nothing happened last night! I wouldn't!" I protested.

He made a dismissive gesture with his hand. "I know that! You're big enough to feel the next day. And you have entirely too many morals."

I blinked at him. Both parts of his statement sounded like praise to me, but he was definitely angry.

"You shouldn't have dragged me out of there!" he snarled, finally being clear.

"I couldn't leave you!" I protested.

I jumped back out of the way as he threw the covers aside and flowed out of bed. He paused for a brief moment, glanced down at the pajamas I had dressed him in, and gave an obvious shudder of distaste. Then his eyes were back on mine.

"Why not? I was having fun!"

I stared at him incredulously. "No, you weren't."

I hadn't imagined the way his eyes were closed, the tiny flinch he had given as the men groped him. I hadn't dreamed his reaction to finding out about the party. I certainly hadn't mistaken the way he had been in bed with me. Eban did not find sex easy to enjoy. Probably due to years of abuse.

"Yes I was!" he exclaimed, putting his hands on his hips and tossing back his long golden hair. "I'm a cock slut."

My jaw dropped and my stomach heaved. Had I been so wrong? Had I created my own little fantasy of how I wanted him to be?

He barged past me, presumably heading for the bathroom. I whirled to watch him go. The image of him wincing in those men's arms played in front of my eyes again. I wasn't wrong. I wasn't crazy.

But Eban had spoken with the courage of conviction. He believed it to be true. He had been taught to believe it about himself. Perhaps it was like the way jerks thought of omegas, disdained them, shamed them for their biological needs. It wouldn't surprise me if people were similarly stupid about vessels. Needing sex was nothing to be ashamed of. It shouldn't be ridiculed or taken advantage of. Just because the body needed it, didn't mean the mind was always happy about it. A body's response was not consent.

Eban thought he was a willing slut because people abused him.

Anger settled over me like a red mist. I chased after him and pushed him face-first up against the wall before standing close behind him. He didn't squirm, didn't fight.

"Tell me no. Tell me to leave you alone. Tell me you don't want to," I snarled into his ear.

Silence. Nothing but his harsh rapid breathing.

I pressed myself closer to his back. "Tell me no, to prove that you can."

He shivered but said nothing.

I released him with a snarl and stepped back. He stayed plastered against the wall where I had shoved him.

"There is nothing wrong with sleeping around because you genuinely enjoy it," I said. "But that's not you. You are not a slut. You've just had all the no's beaten out of you. Not being able to say no, is not the same as saying yes."

Eban sucked in a trembling breath and gave a little sob that broke my heart. Then he pushed himself away from the wall and dashed into the bathroom, slamming the door behind him.

I stared at the closed door in horror as realization of what I had done hit me like a slap in the face. Talk about being an alphahole.

How on earth was he ever going to forgive me?

Chapter Twelve

Avoiding Eban was ridiculously easy. He stayed in his rooms and I stayed in my tiny one next door. I was being a coward again, but I couldn't help it. I lay alone in my bed and listened to him move around. Listened to him drink. Listened to him sing softly to himself. He had a lovely voice.

I realized with dismay that he had nothing to listen to music on. He didn't even have a television. It seemed beyond cruel. What harm could a radio do? It was almost as if Hyde wanted to break him down and drive him crazy.

The day passed slower than treacle oozing off of a spoon. I'd never been happier to see evening roll around. Eban and Hyde had a trip to the theater scheduled in the diary. An opening night of a show Hyde was a patron of.

I knocked on the door to Hyde's office and carefully arranged my features into a blank expression.

"Enter."

He didn't bother to look up from his computer screen as I walked in.

"I just wanted to check the arrangements for the theater, will you have a private box?" I asked in the politest tone I could pull off.

Hyde frowned. "I'm tied up with this, Eban can go alone."

I nodded and quietly shut the door behind me. Bracing myself, I headed for Eban's room. He answered with "Come in," as soon as I knocked.

He was getting ready and peering at himself in the mirror.

"I'm so old!" he exclaimed. "I have wrinkles!"

"You're in your twenties," I stated in confusion. Both at his comment, and the fact he was acting like nothing had happened between us. Like I hadn't pushed him against a wall and said cruel things.

"Late twenties, very late twenties," he corrected. "Before I know it I will be thirty, which will mean my life is half over."

I puzzled over his math. "Humans live for around 90 years."

His gray eyes met mine in the mirror. "Yes, but by the time I'm sixty, I'll be old and shriveled. Wrinkly and ugly and my magic all used up. I'll be no good to anyone. So anything after that is merely lingering, not living."

I blinked at him. "Vessels have a menopause?"

Eban gave a snort laugh and hearing the happy sound flipped my insides over. My wolf perked up and urged me to make Eban laugh again. I agreed it was a wonderful idea but I didn't have the faintest clue where to start. Comedy was not my strong point. Instead, I focused on the task on hand.

"Hyde's not coming to the theater, he said for you to go alone."

"Great," said Eban. I wondered if he was being sarcastic or if he was genuinely pleased.

"Will you have a private box?" I asked.

"Yes," he answered and turned his attention back to brushing his hair.

"We should leave at half-past, the traffic report shows heavier traffic than usual."

"Okay," said Eban with a soft smile as our eyes met in the mirror again.

I nodded and swiftly left. It was fantastic that we could be civil to one another, though why he was offering me that much after what I had done to him, bewildered me. Then like a bucket of ice water hitting me, I realized. Eban was so used to being treated awfully, he thought nothing of it.

I growled, and my fists clenched into tight balls. My tentative good mood washed away. I'd been looking forward to accompanying Eban to the theater, even if it was only as his bodyguard. Now I was just back to feeling ashamed of myself. Hopefully, I would get a chance to at least apologize.

The theater was fancy. It was a proper red carpet event. I held the car door open for Eban and then followed him up the red carpet. He looked like he belonged there. As glamorous as any star. The handful of photographers in attendance rushed to snap him, no doubt trying to figure out who he was.

Eban waltzed past them effortlessly. Like he was used to the attention. He really did not look like a patron.

Staff ushered him to the bar and a champagne reception. I hid my frown as he gracefully took a glass. He really did drink too much. 'When he is ours and happy, he will stop,' my wolf informed me regally. I winced. My inner wolf was an idiot. Eban was never going to be mine.

The lights flickered, indicating that the show was about to start. Eban graciously said farewell to the people he was talking to and made his way upstairs to the private boxes. He seemed to know exactly where he was going and it made me wonder if it was Hyde's permanent box we were heading to.

He opened the door, and I admired the fabulous view of the stage. Eban took his seat, and I took my place standing by the door. A little off center so I could see the stage clearly. The chances of someone barging into the box to harm Eban were slim to none, so I allowed myself the decadence of watching the play.

"I'm not having you loom behind me all evening, sit down," said Eban, as he patted the chair next to him.

I sat down beside him. We were alone in the privacy of the box. The knowledge felt like electricity racing over my skin.

"I'm... so sorry," I said intently, putting all my heart and soul into my words.

Eban gave me a surprised look but seemed to discern what I was babbling about. He sighed.

"It's hard to stay mad at you when you keep rescuing me and carrying me around like a princess and you do things like stay up all night holding my hand."

I stared back at him, hardly daring that he was so very forgiving and feeling quite certain that I did not deserve it. "I've been so mean to you. I called you ugly, got you into trouble with your husband. Yesterday, I assaulted you!"

He gave me a long level look. "You are one of the nicest people I have ever met."

"Says a lot for the company you keep," I grumbled uncomfortably.

He laughed. A warm full laugh. "You might have a point there."

I stared into his bright eyes. How could he be so full of life when his life was so awful? He was too good for this world and he deserved far better.

He tilted his head to the side and regarded me seriously. "Bastion, whilst the delivery wasn't the best, what you said yesterday really helped."

I sucked in a breath at that, suddenly too helpless to do anything but stare back at him.

"More than you'll ever know," he added softly.

I was long out of words, so I took his hand and held it tightly. The lights dimmed and the show began. We watched the whole thing with our hands clasped together in the dark.

After the show, there was more socializing and more champagne. It felt strange to go back to silently standing behind him, after the intimacy of sitting in the box together. My wolf whined, unable to comprehend what had gone wrong.

Eventually the event wrapped up and I helped Eban to the car. He was drunk and giggly but seemed happy and exuberant. Getting out had been good for him.

I sat in the backseat with him. He took my hand again and started gushing about the play we had just watched. His judgment had seemed aloof and reserved when discussing it with the other guests. But here, with me, he babbled enthusiastically about it. I smiled fondly, delighted he had enjoyed himself.

Far too soon, we arrived home. I helped him out of the car. We laughed as we walked up the stairs, arm in arm. Eban swaying slightly.

The footman opened the door to reveal Hyde waiting in the entrance hall. His dark eyes raked over us, lingering on where our arms were joined. Suspicion clouded his features, and I swallowed dryly. Then Eban staggered, losing his balance and I had to steady him. Making it clear I was merely holding his arm because he was drunk.

"I've been waiting for you," snapped Hyde.

"Apologies husband dearest, I'm here now," said Eban brightly.

Hyde frowned, strode up to Eban and grabbed his chin, tilting his head up so he could peer into his eyes.

"You are ripe. Actually on schedule for a change."

"Yes, husband," replied Eban, almost meekly.

Hyde grabbed Eban's free arm and took him away from me. He started marching Eban up the grand staircase, to his room, to... My thoughts stuttered to a halt as my wolf went crazy. Growling, whining, howling. Thrashing around deep inside of me, desperate to get free so it could do something, anything.

But I did not set my wolf free. I didn't do anything. I just turned on my heels and fled. Out of the door and out onto the street. I ran and ran, but as far and as fast as I went, I could not escape a thing.

Chapter Thirteen

I knew Eban was not a morning person, but nevertheless, dawn the next day found me pacing outside his bedchamber. Hyde was long gone, his scent nothing more than a lingering affront that curled my lip. Yet somehow, it did not feel right to barge into Eban's bedroom and check he was alright. I sniffed outside his door, probably a bit dementedly, but I caught no traces of blood or injury.

Eban had slept with his husband. Like he had done a thousand times before. I had no idea why I was feeling so frantic about it.

Except, I did know. I knew how scared Eban had been with me because he expected me to be like Hyde. My wolf growled in rage and before I knew what was happening, I was bursting into Eban's bedchamber and jumping up onto his bed. Desperate to check every inch of him for harm.

Eban scrambled up to a sitting position and stared at me in alarm.

"Are you alright?" I exclaimed.

He gave me a strange look and then frowned. "No. I appear to be awake at an ungodly hour."

"Sorry," I said sheepishly.

Eban sighed and rubbed his hands over his face. Then he looked up at me with a smile.

"Nevermind, tell the staff to bring breakfast, won't you darling?"

I nodded mutely as my heart did cartwheels. I knew he called everyone 'darling' and it meant nothing, but I still loved hearing that term of endearment on his lips.

I scurried off to do his bidding.

After his shower, he came and joined me at the breakfast table. He poured tea, buttered a crumpet and proceeded to chat away about everything and nothing.

I watched him intently, but he seemed fine. It should have been reassuring, but it just made me sad. He appeared fine because nothing unusual had happened. Just another day in the life he had led for ten long years.

"Let's go for a walk," he said suddenly.

I blinked at him in confusion. He had never shown the slightest inclination in being interested in the outdoors.

He caught my look and grinned. "A stroll around an inner city London park is hardly a trek in the wilderness. It will be fresh air and it will just be the two of us."

I could think of nothing better.

Apparently, Eban could get ready lightning fast, if it was just for a walk in the park. He emerged from his dressing room in plain light blue jeans and a gray hoodie. His long blond hair was swept back into a ponytail. He looked more beautiful than I had ever seen him.

Wasting no more time, we made our way outside. The nearest park was only around the corner. It was huge, with wide tree-lined paths. Despite the crisp chill in the air, the day was bright and clear.

Eban linked his arm in mine and I allowed myself to fantasize that we could be like this always.

"This is where all the ton promenade," said Eban.

I raised an eyebrow. "Do people still do that?"

Eban grinned at me. "We are doing it."

I couldn't help returning his smile. Then he sighed dramatically.

"But no, sadly no one does it anymore."

I looked at a middle-aged man in a puffy jacket who was walking opposite us. I nodded in his direction.

"You never know, he could be a duke." He really didn't look like one, but then again Eban in his jeans and hoodie did not look like a lord.

Eban laughed. "Darling, I know everyone," he said, but then he narrowed his eyes. "Although, he does rather look like Duke Hastings. His wife has fled back to the country after catching him with the housekeeper." Eban winked up at me.

"Shocking," I said with a chuckle.

Then I gestured at a young woman pushing a pram. "Isn't that Lady Fancypants? I heard her husband has been overseas for over a year. Terrible that she was pregnant for so very long."

Eban laughed, a rich full musical laugh that made my heart flutter. It was hard to believe that a simple walk in the park was bringing me so much joy.

"Don't look now, but there is Earl Stickuphisass. I heard he lost one of his houses to Lord Sneakygit in a poker game and is absolutely fuming," said Eban as he gestured to a young man jogging in tiny pink shorts.

It was my turn to laugh. A proper, shoulder heaving laugh. Eban smirked at me, his gray eyes sparkling. There was a fondness in his gaze that seized my attention and made it hard to look away.

Eventually, I managed it. Turning my attention to the trees we were passing and trying to get my thoughts in order. Eban could never be mine, but I could stay as his bodyguard for as long as possible. Savor all the stolen moments such as these. I had a sinking feeling that they would not be enough. My wolf would not be satisfied. Neither would

I. But what was the alternative? Resign and walk away? Leave Eban to his unhappy life and never see him again?

My heart clenched painfully at the mere thought. I was so screwed. Stuck between a rock and a hard place with the only options available to me, ones that led to misery and heartache.

I looked at Eban and smiled. Keeping my dark thoughts to myself. This moment was precious and I did not want to waste it. Out here under the autumn sun, all was well. I was walking arm and arm with Eban and talking nonsense. Nothing else mattered.

"Let's go see the ducks," I said suddenly.

I could already picture Eban standing by the sun dappled water. I only wished I had some duck food with me. I was suddenly sure he would love to feed the ducks.

I whipped out my phone and called the butler. "Hargreaves, Lord du Fray would like to feed the ducks, please send someone to meet us with some bread."

"Peas!" injected Eban brightly. "They are healthier for ducks."

Confirming the butler had heard that, I then hung up. Eban was giving me a bemused look.

"What?" I asked.

He shook his head. "Never knew alpha shifters were such softies."

I opened my mouth to protest and then closed it again. He was right. When it came to him I was nothing but a softy and I didn't care.

Chapter Fourteen

We spent hours in the park. Feeding the ducks and then just strolling and chatting. That evening, Eban invited me to have dinner with him in his rooms. I accepted. Probably far too fast. But I didn't care about appearing macho. I wanted Eban to know how I felt about him.

Long after the food was finished, I lingered. The well of conversation never seemed to dry up. Eban laughed and twirled his wineglass, with long, elegant fingers. I could have watched him forever.

At sometime late into the evening, the door behind me opened. Eban's expression told me it was Hyde before my sense of smell did.

Hyde walked into my field of vision and over to the door of Eban's bedchamber. He paused with his hand on the handle and tilted his head at Eban, in a clear 'Get in,' gesture.

I bristled and Eban went deathly pale.

"I'm... I'm not ripe," said Eban softly, and it broke my heart to hear him stutter.

"I'm aware of that," said Hyde coldly.

"You never..." began Eban before trailing off.

"I'm aware of that too," answered Hyde, his dark eyes boring straight into me and causing my world to end. Eban was Hyde's vessel, he had to obey him. In all things. Marital sex was just another obligation.

I jumped to my feet, balling my hands into fists in an effort to contain my snarling wolf. Hyde was asserting his dominance. Making a point. And putting me in my place by taking Eban to bed in front of me.

I had stepped over the line, and Eban was going to pay the price for it.

Hyde didn't mind me sleeping with Eban when it was convenient for him, but he clearly didn't like me getting close to him. Hyde wasn't going to let his husband have a relationship. It was a threat to his control over Eban.

I stared back at Hyde, and he smirked at me in satisfaction. He knew I couldn't do anything, knew I didn't want to lose my job and never see Eban again. Hyde enjoyed having control over me as well as his husband. He liked power. He seemed to thrive on it.

Eban climbed gracefully to his feet, hung his head and shuffled into his bedchamber. Hyde smiled at me, stepped in and closed the door in my face.

I stared at the closed door for a split second before sucking in a desperate breath, turning on my heels and fleeing. I ran out of the house and pounded the streets of London all night. Hours and hours passed and still I raged. My wolf demanding we challenge Hyde for what we wanted. But Hyde wasn't a shifter and the human world did not work like that. Problems could rarely be solved with fights.

As the dawn light began to illuminate the city, I headed back. I knew what I needed to do. Keep my distance from Eban. Be his bodyguard and nothing more. Keep him safe. Stay away from him in order to protect him from his husband. I could do no more. I couldn't be Eban's friend. Hyde had me exactly where he wanted me and he had Eban exactly where he wanted him. Alone. Isolated. Fully under Hyde's power.

And there was not a thing I could do about it.

I jogged into the house. Still anxious and on edge despite my long night. I got to my room, shut the door and started pacing. A few seconds later the scents hit me. Eban had been sick. A lot.

Heart hammering frantically, I burst into his bedchamber. He was sprawled half on the bed, half off. His head dangling. I rushed over to him and cradled his head. His skin was pale and clammy. His eyes didn't open and he lolled bonelessly in my arms.

My gaze fell onto the empty bottle of pills and the empty bottle of vodka. I swore vehemently. Guilt and horror gnawing at me. I should never have left him alone.

I pulled the bell rope hanging by the bed. The valet appeared, eyes growing huge as he took in the scene.

"Is there a healer on staff?"

"Ah...No."

I swore. "Get Hyde."

"His lordship left late last night."

Cold ice clenched my guts. I had no magic of my own. I couldn't heal him. And he really needed a healer. Eban was far too pale, far too limp.

My mind scrambled frantically for options on what to do. Then I realized. He had magic but he was still human.

"Call an ambulance!" I snapped.

"But.."

"Just do it!" I growled. There wasn't time for arguments about never involving mundanes in paranormal matters. Even human paranormals weren't supposed to go to hospital, in case the tests revealed something. But I couldn't care less. I would not let Eban die.

The ambulance came mercifully quickly. I wondered if it was being called to an exclusive address in Mayfair, or if they were always that swift.

Stepping away from Eban to let the paramedics work was one of the hardest things I had ever had to do. My wolf did not want to let him go.

"What's his name?" asked one of the paramedics.

"Eban," I croaked.

"Eban? Eban, can you hear me?" he said loudly.

Eban did not respond. There was not even the faintest fluttering of his eyelids. I swallowed dryly. An oxygen mask was slipped over his face. They put a needle in his arm and attached a bag of fluids. Then they moved him onto the trolley. He looked so helpless.

"Is that what he took?" asked the paramedic, gesturing at the empty bottle of pills.

"I... I think so. But I don't know for sure." I hated being so useless.

The paramedic nodded, grabbed the bottle and put it on the trolley with Eban. Presumably to show the doctor at the hospital.

They pushed the trolley along at a careful yet agonizingly slow speed. Then they got to the top of the stairs.

"Let me help!" I snapped impatiently.

"Sorry, we can't do that."

I growled, stepped forward and picked up the trolley holding Eban. It was nothing for my alpha strength. I ran down the stairs and then across the entrance hall, before running down the short flight of stairs outside the house. I set it gently down on the pavement by the ambulance. The paramedics had chased after me and were now staring at me wide eyed.

"I... um work out a lot and... adrenaline." I shrugged.

Their faces softened and one of them patted me kindly on the arm.

"You must really care for him."

I drew in a shaky breath. I did. I really did. Even more than I had known.

They bundled Eban into the ambulance. I scrambled in after them and tried not to cry. Everything had suddenly turned so awful. A Thousand times worse than it had been a few hours ago. The shock and the speed of the change left me reeling.

Thankfully, the journey passed quickly. As soon as we arrived at the hospital, they whisked him away. Leaving me to pace distraughtly in the hallway. If Eban was okay, I'd never whine about having to keep my distance from him again. As long as he was in the world, I could cope with anything.

After the longest hour of my life, they let me in. Eban was lying on a bed, hooked up to a dizzying array of machines. He was still out cold, looking so defenseless that it nearly broke my soul. My wolf wanted to leap up onto the bed and curl around him protectively.

The doctor talked to me but the only words I really heard were, "He is going to be okay."

Sagging in relief, I pulled up a chair to his bedside and clasped his hand. This had all been my fault. I'd left him to suffer his husband alone. Acting like the injured party, when I should have manned up, put my own angst aside and been there for him after Hyde left.

Hyde only using him when he was ripe was likely Eban's one small solace in ten years of hell. No wonder losing that one tiny grace had been the last straw.

Eban's eyes opened and my heart went crazy. I tightened my grip on his hand. He looked up at me, beautiful eyes all hazy and confused. Impulsively, I brought his hand up to my lips and kissed it. He blinked at me.

"You came back," he said softly, an incredulous look on his face.

"I never left," I reassured him calmly, while my very soul was shattering from the force of his words.

He had thought I had gone for good. He hadn't known I had just gone for a walk, he had believed I had left him and was never going to come back. I'd been such a selfish, stupid idiot.

Images of him going to my room, upset and crying after Hyde's departure, only to find it empty and then hearing from the staff that I was nowhere to be found, clawed at my mind until I wanted to howl in anguish.

"Oh," he whispered.

His eyes fluttered again and he drifted back to sleep. But he looked far more peaceful this time. I watched his steady breathing for a while, then I bowed my head and sobbed.

It was far worse than I had thought. It wasn't Hyde that had driven him to this. It was me. I had led him to believe it was more than I could bear. That I wasn't willing to put up with Hyde. I had made him feel like he was all alone in the world. I wasn't sure if I would ever be able to forgive myself.

Chapter Fifteen

Later that day, Eban woke up properly. He still looked pale and drawn.

I clasped his hand in both of mine. "I'm sorry," I breathed passionately.

He smiled softly at me and raised his free hand to tenderly caress my face.

"You showed me everything I can never have," he said.

It felt like my soul was shattering into a thousand jagged, broken shards, but I smiled at him and shifted the conversation to small talk. He was clearly still woozy, and I didn't want him to say something he would regret or be embarrassed about later.

He responded to my meaningless conversation, but then we mostly sat in companionable silence. There were a million things I wanted to say, but I didn't want to hound him the moment he was conscious, and it was just so wonderful that he had recovered, I wanted to savor the moment.

He was awake and here, with me. I was holding his hand. It was enough. It would always be enough.

Not long after he had woken up, a short woman with a bright smile and a clipboard walked in. She glanced down at mine and Eban's clasped hands.

"Can I talk to Eban alone please?"

Eban tightened his grip on my hand. "No, it's okay, you can talk freely in front of him."

Her gaze hardened. "I'm afraid I must insist. It won't take long."

I got to my feet, kissed the top of his head and reluctantly reclaimed my hand. I was glad she was checking if I was an abusive boyfriend. It meant the hospital was being thorough in their care of Eban. Maybe they could uncover the truth about Hyde and save Eban from him.

I lurked just outside the door and realized far too late that it was thin enough for my shifter hearing to hear everything.

"Your boyfriend is a big man, is he hurting you?"

"He's not my boyfriend, he is my bodyguard."

A slight pause. "The nature of some of your injuries..."

"That was someone else."

My stomach heaved. Hyde had hurt in more than one way. And Eban sounded so uncomfortable talking about it, I longed to storm back in there and throw the woman out.

"Do you want to talk to the police?"

"No."

Another pause. "Eban, did you plan to do what happened last night?"

"No." Eban's voice sounded certain and my heart did a little skip of joy. "I just got stupidly drunk and was very upset."

"Okay, I'd still like someone from the mental health team to do a full assessment before you are discharged later today. Is that alright?"

Eban must have nodded, because she continued.

"Great. I'll get the nurse to remove your drip and the monitors."

With that, the door opened and she brushed past me. I rushed back in, reclaiming my seat and his hand.

"Everything okay?" I asked, feeling guilty for eavesdropping.

He nodded. "Yes, I should be able to go home later today."

I smiled softly at him. I didn't mind that he didn't want to tell me everything. He was entitled to his privacy. It just made me feel worse for spying on him. I was a little disappointed that it seemed like he wasn't going to tell them about Hyde, but it had only been a foolish hope. Wanting mundanes to come and fix everything was ridiculous.

A short while later a nurse came in and gently slid the needle out of his arm. Then she disconnected him from the machines that were measuring his heart rate and oxygen levels.

After she left, the room felt strangely quiet without the gentle beeping. I phoned the butler and asked him to send someone with clothes for Eban. His had vanished somewhere and had been in a sorry state when I had last seen them, anyway. He'd be more comfortable out of the hospital gown and it wasn't like he could wear that flimsy cloth home.

It didn't take long for a footman to arrive. I closed the curtain around the bed and Eban swiftly got dressed. Seeing him in plain jeans and a tee shirt was soothing. He looked more like his normal self. He didn't look like a hospital patient anymore.

A few heartbeats later Hyde stormed in. His expensive suit was very slightly crumpled, but his perfectly black, knee-length tailored coat screamed wealth. He had two muscled henchmen I had never seen before with him.

Without a word, Hyde grabbed Eban by the arm and marched him out of the room. I hastened after, as Hyde strode through the ward with him. Several staff members looked up in alarm. One nurse scurried after him.

"He has not been discharged yet."

"I do not need a doctor's permission to take my husband home," snarled Hyde.

The nurse wilted and stopped in her tracks. Giving up her pursuit. I stared around at the other staff but it was obvious no one was going to say anything. It was clear they could sense his wealth and social power and I wondered if some part of them could also sense his magic.

Whatever the reason, we made it outside without being challenged. It was a prime example of Hyde's power and a demonstration of his ownership over Eban. It filled me with dismay. It seemed likely that Hyde could just as easily haul Eban out of a police station. Eban was completely trapped. Owned. Possessed. Nothing but property.

Hyde shoved Eban into the backseat of his car. The henchmen climbed into their own car that was parked right behind Hyde's. I scrambled to climb in next to the driver before anyone noticed me. It was uncertain if I still had a job. Calling an ambulance had been a bold move.

"No!" snapped Hyde as he glared at me.

I winced.

"In the back with us," he ordered.

Hardly daring to believe my luck, I hurried to obey. As soon as I shut the door behind me, the car sped off. Eban pressed himself against the other door and stared out of the window as if he could pretend he wasn't there. Hyde ignored him in return and focused on me instead.

"What did the hospital say?"

"Physically, he is going to be fine. We got there in time. He needs rest and fluids."

Hyde nodded his comprehension. I could see in his eyes that he understood my emphasis on the word physically.

"Thank you," Hyde said curtly.

I felt my eyebrows rise in surprise. Then I realized that Eban was very expensive property. Hyde was thanking me for protecting his assets. The man hadn't suddenly grown a heart.

Hyde huffed out a breath, and I noticed for the first time how pale and tired he looked. I pictured him flying halfway around the world before having to jump on the next plane back.

"I take it they didn't discover his magic?"

"No."

He gave me a strange look. "I know I'm not a good man, but I'd never want to be a murderer."

I stared at him in shock before mutely nodding my head. Of all the things I thought he might have said, that would never have appeared in my wildest imaginings.

Hyde glanced at Eban, who was still resolutely staring out of the window and ignoring us completely.

"I went too far and for that, I apologize," he said, continuing with the surprises.

There was nothing I could say to that. It was not my place to accept his apology. He shouldn't even be voicing it to me. Talking to me as if Eban wasn't there, made it clear Hyde considered me a man and Eban property. It made me like him even less, even though he was apologizing. Personally, I thought what he had done was unforgivable. Thankfully, he didn't seem affronted by my silence.

"I wouldn't care, but it disturbs his magic. I cannot allow it," stated Hyde blandly.

My mouth opened and shut several times before the words would come.

"We are not having an affair," I declared.

"But you want to," he replied calmly.

I flushed at that. I hoped Eban wanted that, but I didn't know for sure. I wasn't sure if I wanted to know. Both answers carried pain. Yes, would be bittersweet. No, would be rejection. I was in too deep to be able to respond rationally to either.

It was shameful that it was so easy for Hyde to read me. He knew I wanted Eban when I had only recently begun to fully acknowledge it myself. I'd sworn to Hyde that I'd never fall for a human and he had believed me and hired me.

I understood why Hyde had been pissed off, it still didn't excuse him though. Hurting Eban was unforgivable. I had no idea why I wasn't ripping his throat out. Probably because my guilty heart knew Eban had been more upset by what I had done, than what Hyde had. I carried more of the blame. Eban had needed me and I hadn't been there.

"It cannot happen," continued Hyde ruthlessly. Pulling my thoughts back to our conversation. "Other than times I'm away and he is ripe."

It should have been a glimmer of hope. Something to hold on to, to look forward to. But it just filled me with misery. I wanted to be with Eban. I wanted to share my life with him. It wasn't about sex. Especially as sex was complicated for Eban. I just wanted Eban to be mine. To be my mate. I wanted to fall asleep with him in my arms and wake up with him still there. I did not want nothing more than the occasional hook up.

Hyde attempting to be reasonable was worse than him being an ass. It made it clear that there was no hope for us. Even if he was happy to give us his blessing, he could not.

Eban and I could never be together.

Chapter Sixteen

The next few days passed gently as Eban slowly regained his sparkle. Returning to his usual flirtatious, vivacious ways. It pained me to think it might be just an act. Walls. Armor. A barrier between us. But if they made him feel stronger, I needed to accept it.

I'd been privileged to see the softer, more gentle Eban. I wanted to see more of him, but more than that I wanted to regain his trust. I'd left him in his darkest hour and he had believed I'd left him forever. I needed to show him that would never happen. No matter how dark things got, I was here for the long haul. I would never abandon him again. Wolves were loyal.

We were having breakfast together in his rooms, when suddenly he spilled coffee on himself. He jumped to his feet with an impressive list of swear words.

"Are you okay?" I asked anxiously.

He held his coffee soak pajama top away from his skin.

"Yeah, I'm fine," he muttered without looking at me.

He wasn't a morning person at the best of times. It wasn't surprising his coffee accident was souring his mood. I was just glad he was unhurt.

"You kiss your mom with that mouth?" I teased.

He walked away from me, towards the bathroom.

"I've never kissed anyone," he mumbled distractedly.

I watched him go and puzzled over his words. That couldn't be right? What was he on about? How could he have never kissed anyone?

I got to my feet and paced. Agitation itching down my spine. My wolf restless and rattled. He had to be lying. Why was he lying to me, now, after everything we had been through? And why lie over something like this?

The last few days had been a torment. His smell. His laugh. The way he tucked his hair behind his ear. He captivated me and I wanted him. Longed for him. But couldn't have him.

I thought he had been feeling the same. I thought I had seen it in his eyes and his lingering glances. As well as in the way he made easy excuses for us to spend nearly every waking moment together.

Was he just teasing me? Playing me? Why else would he make up such a ridiculous story? Was I nothing more than a game to him?

Eban walked back into the room, wearing clean clothes and smelling divine.

I pounced, pushing him back against the wall. My hand twined into Eban's silky long hair, pulling his head up and angling it just right. I was going to kiss him and he was going to kiss me back passionately, proving his lie.

I lowered my head and kissed him. Eban's lips were so soft, warm, and the taste of him ignited a fire in my belly.

Eban didn't move, standing stock still but I could smell his arousal. I licked the seam of his mouth and he whimpered hungrily but didn't part his lips, didn't kiss me back.

I didn't give up, instead I kissed him deeper, harder. His lips finally parted and he tentatively, clumsily attempted to follow my lead.

With a growl, I broke the kiss. I didn't release him from the wall or remove my hand from his hair. I stared deep into those gray eyes.

"How come you don't know how to kiss?" I demanded. My thoughts all jumbled in an incoherent mess.

Eban stared back at me, his gray eyes swirling with emotion. "I've never done it before," he said simply.

I did release him then and backed away to pace back and forth. How could it be true? Eban's husband had never kissed him? In ten years of marriage? Not one of the people Eban had been made to take to his bed, ever cared for him, or wanted anything more than to take his body? But I was to blame too. I had not kissed him either.

It was infuriating, it was wrong. My wolf wanted to destroy them all, even though I was also to blame. Then another thought dawned on me and I swore.

"I thought you were lying," I snapped.

Eban flinched, still standing plastered against the wall where I had left him. I felt a flash of guilt and tried to explain.

"I didn't want that to be your first kiss." I gestured helplessly at him, trying to indicate what I had done.

Eban smiled softly. "I did."

I could only stare helplessly. Every word I had ever learned somehow fell out of my mind. Shortly followed by the ability to form a single coherent thought.

Eban's gaze grew more intense. "Teach me," he whispered. His gray eyes holding me prisoner.

My mind whirled, the thought of teaching Eban to kiss made me giddy. Slowly I shook my head and remembered how to speak.

"No, that should be someone you love."

Eban held my gaze intently. The slightest hint of a nod of agreement.

"Teach me," he breathed again.

The next thing I knew, I had him in my arms. Exactly where my wolf was adamant he belonged. But I wasn't teaching Eban, I was devouring him. Kissing him desperately, needily. As if I was ravenous and he was the only source of nourishment in the world.

His arms rose up to twine around my neck and he moaned, pressing his whole body against mine. I put my hands around his hips and hoisted him up. He quickly understood and wrapped his long legs around my waist. Now I didn't need to lean down to kiss him. I could hold him against the wall and plunder his mouth even deeper than before.

"Finally!" huffed my wolf in giddy excitement.

"Stop," Eban gasped.

I stopped but did not let go of him. The fabric of his sweatpants was not thick enough to hide the firmness of his cock that was pressing into my stomach.

"We can't," he said, staring at me with his pupils blown and I knew he wasn't talking about kissing. It was clear we were both getting too carried away to be satisfied just with kisses.

"What can we do?" I asked.

I understood that penetrative sex would mess with his magic and make his cycle unpredictable. As well as create other magical issues that I could not comprehend. But there were many other ways to make love. I was more than happy to explore them all.

Eban stared at me dazedly. I realized he was far too flummoxed to answer me.

"Can I give you a blow job?" I suggested helpfully.

He flushed beautifully and he nodded shyly. Grinning, I let him slide his feet down to the floor, then I hurriedly dropped to my knees, yanking his trousers down to his, in almost the same move.

He chuckled, and the soft sound was full of amusement, surprise, nervousness and desire. It rippled through my soul and flared my arousal.

Wasting no more time, I greedily swallowed him whole. He cried out, rising up on his toes.

I nearly peaked right then and there, just from his reaction. But diligently I kept going. Experimenting with different levels of suction and rhythm until I discovered a combination that had him moaning beautifully.

His cock was firm in my mouth, and the taste of him was exquisite. The feel of him on my tongue was ecstasy. I could have stayed there on my knees pleasuring him for hours. But he was close, very close, and I wanted to see him undone.

I slid my head up until only the very tip of him was in my mouth. Then I swiped my tongue across his slit, pushing down with slight pleasure before diving all the way down again, taking him into my throat. I swallowed around him and he exploded. The cry he made as he spilled down my throat was the most erotic noise I had ever heard. I wanted to hear it every day. Several times a day.

A feeling like static danced along every inch of my skin, it sunk into my being, creating a glorious, dizzying rush of euphoria. It was his magic. Insanely aroused as I was, it was enough to tip me over the edge and I came in my underwear. Untouched.

I leaned back on my heels and looked up at him. His face was flushed and beautiful, but his eyes were full of alarm. He bit his bottom lip.

"Maybe he won't notice?" I said hopefully.

It didn't feel like all his magic. It wasn't as intense as when we had had sex. Hopefully, it was just a little. Not enough to earn Hyde's ire. Hyde had seemed to rescind his objection about Eban I getting close. For fear of breaking his vessel. And the man had made it perfectly clear that as long as Eban's magic was untouched, he didn't care what we did.

Eban nodded even though he didn't look convinced. It tore at my heart to see him look so worried. But there wasn't anything we could do about it now. What was done was done. The only thing I could do was comfort him.

I rose to my feet, pulled his trousers up and scooped him into my arms. I carried him into his bedroom and placed him on his bed. I did a quick maneuver where I shucked off my pants, removed my soiled underwear before pulling my pants back on commando.

Then I climbed in with him, pulling him in close as the little spoon.

He lay there, every muscle in his body tense.

"What are you doing?" he asked after a while.

"Snuggling," I said, taking a big sniff of his hair and sighing happily. "Can't accidentally take your magic by snuggling."

"So what? We just lie here?" he asked, sounding very skeptical.

"Yeah," I murmured as I tightened my arm around his waist.

Very slowly, he relaxed. I could almost feel the tension in his body drifting away.

"This is quite nice actually," he admitted.

If I had been in wolf form my tail would have been wagging crazily in delight. Making Eban feel safe and happy was wonderful. I just needed to do more of it. Every day. More and more, until everything was alright.

Chapter Seventeen

I wanted to stay curled up in bed together all day, but Eban had other ideas. He got up and went for a swim followed by some yoga. I didn't need to watch him, but I did. It was nice to see how he earned his fabulous body. It was even more wonderful just to spend time with him.

Then it was time to get ready for an event at an art gallery. It was hard to get back into the mindset of being just his bodyguard again. I knew I needed to behave impeccably. Hyde would be watching. He would be pissed off if anything was obvious. Gossips didn't need much to start a scandal. As much as Hyde didn't care personally, I knew he would not tolerate being subjected to ridicule.

I told myself that I was a professional and that I could do it. I needed to do it if I wanted to keep my job and be near Eban.

As we entered the art gallery, I concentrated on keeping a measured three steps away from Eban. He grabbed a drink off of the tray a passing server was holding and launched straight into conversation with a group of people.

Hyde wandered off to talk to a different group. My eyes fell upon the art on display. It was hideous. Why anyone would want it on their walls was beyond me. It was probably a good thing the prices weren't displayed or else I might have had a seizure.

Eban's little crowd drifted away but he wasn't standing alone for long. A young man, all but bounced up to him. He had short, very curly hair that was an attractive deep red. His eyes were large and brown. Freckles painted his face. With his short and very slender frame, he was the epitome of cute. It made me realize how smitten I was, because I couldn't fully appreciate his good looks.

"Cousin!" he beamed brightly at Eban.

"Colby," replied Eban with an air of great resignation.

Colby's gaze flicked to me, and his eyes widened. "Why is your bodyguard so hot!" he exclaimed. "It's not fair!"

Eban said nothing but I could picture him rolling his eyes.

"Seriously, what is Hyde thinking? And why don't my parents' think like that, instead of lumping me with Denise. Don't suppose you want to swap?" he said, gesturing at a short, very muscled woman in her forties.

Her salt and pepper hair was shaved into a buzz cut. I could tell by her stance she knew her stuff. She was standing across the room, looking like she wasn't paying the slightest bit of attention, but I could tell her focus was fully on her charge.

"Maybe," drawled Eban, snapping my attention back to him in outrage.

He leaned in close to his cousin but I heard every word.

"She looks like she really knows how to fuck. You wouldn't forget getting pegged by her in a hurry."

Colby's eyes grew huge and his hand flew up to his mouth in an effort to hide his shocked giggle.

"Eban!" he admonished gleefully.

Then he sighed dramatically "I might have to settle for that, I'm never going to be married! I'm twenty now! Who ever heard of an unwed vessel at twenty. No one wants me. I will never forgive Lord Waterbury for doing this to me!"

Eban shook his head. "He died in a car crash."

"Two days before our wedding!" gasped Colby as if it were the most shocking inconvenience ever to have befallen a person. "All these years later, I'm still suffering the consequences!"

I recalled that traditionally vessels were married on their eighteenth birthday. Something Colby seemed disgruntled to have missed out on.

"Don't be in such a hurry to be married. Enjoy your youth," said Eban.

Colby huffed in obvious disagreement. "I've got my eyes on Duke Rakewell. He is the most eligible bachelor in society. Please introduce us so I can swoon and he can catch me in his arms."

Eban sighed wearily. "Colby, you are an idiot. I'm not introducing you."

Just then Hyde walked over. Eban politely turned his attention to his husband.

"Is Sothbridge here yet?" asked Hyde.

"Not that I've seen," replied Eban.

"Good evening, my lord," gushed Colby brightly with a little bow and a big bright smile.

Hyde's gaze ran over him. "Evening," he replied with a nod before going on his way.

As soon as he had disappeared into the crowd, Eban grabbed Colby's arm.

"Do not flirt with Hyde!" he hissed angrily.

Colby's eyes widened. "I wouldn't try to steal your husband! I want a marriage, not an affair!"

Eban let go of his arm. "That's not... you're an idiot Colby. You keep playing with fire, you're going to get burned."

Colby scowled and rubbed his arm. Even though I was sure Eban hadn't grabbed him that hard.

"I'm serious Colby, you're young, pretty, untapped. If you are not careful, someone is going to take what you don't want to give."

Colby beamed up at him. "You think I'm pretty?"

Eban growled in exasperation. "Go away Colby, before I hit you!"

Still grinning, Colby walked away. Eban watched him go. I could sense his concern. His frustration. His dismay.

"Denise has all the sense he lacks. She'll make sure he is safe," I said.

Eban glanced up at me in surprise before sighing heavily.

"I hope you are right," he said.

He paused for a moment and took a big sip of his drink.

"One day soon he is going to get what he thinks he wants. He will be married off to a mage and I'll bump into him at one of these things and... all his sparkle will be gone."

Eban's shoulders slumped and he looked so sad. My arms ached to hold him. To comfort him and shield him from the world. But instead I could only offer words.

"He might find a nice husband?" I suggested.

Eban looked up at me with a sad look. "Maybe."

A couple approached and Eban turned to them with a gleaming smile. Slipping back into his role effortlessly. I forced myself back into mine and went back to being his silent shadow, who could only watch him.

That night I was lying alone in my bed trying to sleep when the door that connected our rooms quietly opened. Eban hesitated in the doorway.

Silently, I lifted up my covers. He drifted across the carpet and climbed into bed with me. I put the covers over us and pulled him into a spoon. Sighing happily.

"Shall I give you a blow job?" he asked, his whole body vibrating with tension.

"The only thing I need from you is your time," I said, sniffing his hair.

Eban exhaled, and it was as if it took every molecule of stress from his body. Suddenly he was all relaxed, warm and happy in my arms.

He yawned. "Maybe I won't have any nightmares."

I kissed the top of his head. Here in my bed, I could protect him from all things. Even dark dreams.

Chapter Eighteen

A few days later and it felt like I was in a living nightmare. The ball Eban was attending faded into the background as my attention focused compulsively on Eban and the man he was flirting with. They were sitting with legs touching on a chaise lounge. Apparently completely engrossed with each other.

Hyde stood a few feet away, whisky in hand, talking to some woman. He glanced over frequently, checking on Eban's progress. He had brought the mundane business man over to introduce him to Eban. And Eban had clearly understood the assignment.

The businessman's hand moved to rest on Eban's thigh. I bristled. My wolf snarling and growling within me. 'Mine,' it raged. I did not know how to argue against its assertion.

"Why don't you go out onto the balcony for some fresh air? I'll join you in a moment?" whispered Eban as he leaned in close to the man's ear.

The man smirked and quickly dashed off to do his bidding.

"Stop glowering!" snapped Eban as he took a sip of his drink. He didn't look at me.

I couldn't find the words. My fury was barely contained. Hyde needing Eban's magic was one thing, pimping Eban out for business deals was quite another. I knew he did it. The whole orgy situation had taught me that, but confronted with it again, the only thought in my head was, how dare he?

Eban rose to his feet and ambled nonchalantly towards the balcony. I trailed after him.

"Stop being ridiculous! It's just a blow job," he hissed.

But I couldn't stop it and I didn't think it was ridiculous.

"We need to keep Hyde happy, so he leaves us alone."

He was right but my wolf didn't care.

Eban sighed sorrowfully. "Don't make this harder for me."

Shame doused me like a bucket of cold water. I was being an ass. It wasn't like I was the one having to suck a stranger off, yet I was acting like the one who was hard done by. My feet haltered to a stop. We had reached the balcony. I forced myself to turn around. To stare blindly out at the ballroom.

Eban flashed me a quick glance as he passed me. A look of such pain, it made me catch my breath.

"I'm giving you everything I can," he said softly and then he was gone.

I knew he was, and it was enough. It would have to be. It was this or nothing. Really nothing, as in never even seeing him ever again. When it came to Eban, I'd take the crumbs from the table. They were delicious and precious and I'd cherish them forever.

After what felt like a millennium, the businessman sauntered out of the balcony with a broad satisfied grin on his face. My wolf snarled and wanted to chase after him. I winced as the tips of my claws descended and cut into my palm. The shock of the physical pain brought me to my senses. Fear swirled through me, I'd never lost control and nearly shifted before. I needed to get a grip.

Eban walked out of the balcony. He didn't look at me. Instead, he strode passed me, clearly on his way somewhere. I hurried after him.

He went downstairs and out of some large glass double doors. They led to a large patio that was covered by a canopy. Outdoor heaters were dotted around, fighting against the chill of the night air. Rain dripped off the canopy creating a curtain to the garden that was out there somewhere in the darkness.

A handful of people were dotted around smoking. Eban strode up to a vacant heater. I watched in astonishment as he pulled a packet of cigarettes out of his pocket and lit one. I had never seen him smoke before or even smelled it on him.

A gust of wind flapped the wet canopy. Two smokers hurried back inside. I looked around the nearly empty space. Eban was smoking for cover. So we could be alone. I wondered where he had got the cigarettes from and grimaced. Had he asked the businessman for them? It was quick thinking and resourceful if he had, but my wolf still hated the idea.

"Sorry," mumbled Eban sadly, his eyes fixed on the floor.

"Eban, no! I'm sorry! I was being an asshole."

He took a long drag on his cigarette, while still looking down.

"Please look at me," I begged.

Slowly his beautiful eyes raised to mine and the misery I saw in them caused me to sob out loud. I stepped up close to him, tenderly holding his chin, so he didn't drop his gaze again. I wanted him to see how sorry I was. He needed to see I wasn't going to be a jerk about it. It wasn't his choice or his fault and I was not going to blame him for it. It didn't change how I felt about him. Nothing ever would.

"Eban?" someone called.

I snatched my hand back from his face and hurriedly stepped back from him, But it wasn't quick enough. A young man with floppy brown hair stared at us.

"S... Sorry," he stuttered nervously.

"Charlie!" exclaimed Eban brightly as he strode up to the newcomer and threw his arms around him.

Eban seemed to squish the young man to death. Then he stepped back but kept his hands on Charlie's shoulders.

"You look fabulous, I take it Hathbury is treating you well?"

Charlie flushed and beamed. "Oh, very well!" he gushed as his eyes filled with so much soppy love that my pang of jealousy stole my breath away.

"I thought you hated these things?" asked Eban, gesturing at the house.

"I do!" admitted Charlie easily. "But I was hoping to run into you."

"Oh darling! You are such a sweetheart," said Eban.

Charlie cast me a nervous glance. "How are you, Eban?"

"Never better!"

A small frown furrowed Charlie's brow. "You always say that."

I couldn't stop my grin. I liked this young man. He cared enough about Eban to look a little deeper.

"Do you think your husband would let you come and visit us next week?" blurted out Charlie suddenly, before Eban had a chance to defend his statement about being fine.

"I can ask him," said Eban, sounding puzzled.

"Lord Garrington and Mr. Montfort will be there, I mean, Xander and Fen. But you don't have to tell your husband that."

Charlie looked around the smoking shelter warily, as if there were spies in the shadows, and I realized he had waited until Eban was alone before approaching.

"We have so much to tell you," he whispered.

Eban cast me a quick puzzled glance. "Okay, I'll ask Hyde."

"Great!" said Charlie with a happy nod. "Let me give you my number."

He fished the latest iPhone model out of his pocket. I glanced at Eban before getting my phone out. Charlie didn't need to know that Eban didn't have one.

"Give it to me," I said gruffly.

Charlie blinked at me in surprise but gave me his number without comment. I gave him mine, and he nodded happily as he typed it into his phone. He looked around nervously again.

"Um... I better be going. Hopefully see you soon," he said and darted off.

"What was that about?" I asked as I watched him go.

Eban shrugged. "No idea, but I'm intrigued."

I turned my attention back to Eban. "He saw us."

"He won't say anything, Charlie is a sweetheart," said Eban confidently.

I hoped he was right. As I constantly reminded myself, Hyde might not care what we did, as long as Eban's magic was untouched, but I knew without a doubt that he would not tolerate rumors about his husband having an affair with a bodyguard. Image was everything and powerful men thrived on the illusion that their power was absolute and that they were obeyed in all things.

Charlie did seem like a nice kid and I trusted Eban's judgment, so I put it from my mind. Fretting never helped anyone. Besides, there were more important things to be concerned about.

"Are you okay?" I asked softly.

Eban looked up at me in surprise. He knew I was talking about what had happened on the balcony, not the encounter with Charlie. I saw a flash of something in his eyes and then his expression was carefully blank. He nodded sharply and took a drag of his cigarette.

I wasn't fooled. I longed to wrap my arms around him and hold him close. But we were in public. People could walk in at any minute. As Charlie had shown. It meant we couldn't even hold hands.

"We should go back in," said Eban as he flicked the half smoked cigarette onto the floor and stomped on it with his foot.

I nodded helplessly. He was right, as usual. There was nothing I could do but trail after him, as silent as a shadow.

Chapter Nineteen

Later that night, while Eban was in the shower, I made myself comfortable in his bed. It was a nice bed. Huge, soft and most importantly, despite the clean sheets, his scent was everywhere. I wanted to roll around in it. Rub him into my skin and leave my scent mixed with his all over the bed. Luckily, I managed to control myself. I didn't think Eban was ready for full on shifter behavior yet.

He walked into the bedroom wearing white satin pajamas, and towel drying his hair. He stopped in his tracks when he saw me. His eyes wide and surprised.

"Your bed is bigger than mine," I said, suddenly feeling awkward.

Had I presumed too much? Was I being pushy? He had been slipping into my bed every night for few nights now. Sleeping with him in my arms was sheer bliss, and he had been sleeping soundly, no sign of any night terrors. But that didn't mean he wanted to do it every night. Or wanted to do it in his bed.

But I longed to hold him. I wanted him to forget about the ball and all the unpleasantness. And his bed really was bigger.

"Is this okay?" I asked.

He nodded and threw the towel onto the back of a chair. Grinning in delight, I peeled back the covers so he could climb in.

He looked at me and his eyes went even wider. His cheeks flushed and I heard him swallow. It looked like he was frozen to the spot.

My grin grew even wider. I loved that the sight of my naked body could do that to him. His gaze rove up and down my body several times. Lingering on some places longer than others.

"You don't just have to look," I suggested softly.

He bit his bottom lip. "You're so handsome."

"So are you."

He shook his head and gave a gentle smile. "No, I'm pretty." He gestured at my body. "You're all muscles and man."

"You like it?" I asked.

"Very much," he chuckled.

"Come and join me then."

Eyes sparkling, he did just that. His warm lithe body slid right up to mine. I wrapped my arms around him and stared into his eyes. Happiness exploded inside my chest. Eban in my arms was everything I wanted.

"Can I kiss you?" I breathed huskily.

His gaze dropped to my lips and he nodded. Wasting no more time, I pressed my mouth against his and exulted in the taste of him. His lips were so soft, so warm. A moan rose up from my throat. My tongue slipped inside his mouth. He whimpered hungrily, pressing his entire body even closer. My hands roamed over his body, coming to rest on his wonderful, pert ass. The satin pajamas were nice but I needed his skin. I plucked at the cloth.

"Can these come off?" I asked breathlessly.

For an answer he started wriggling out of them. I helped, and in no time at all he was back pressed against me. His skin against my own, as it should be.

My lips went back to his, my hands back to his ass. But everything was so much better now that he was naked.

I kissed him some more. Thoroughly, deeply, intensely. I wanted him to forget everything but me. I wanted to be his universe. It was working. He was moaning happily in my arms. The scent of his arousal washing over me as his hard cock pressed into my stomach.

I groaned hungrily. I needed more of him. I needed all of him. Our bodies should be melded together as one until we didn't know where one ended and the other began.

The idea I had been mulling over for days, seemed right. It was perfect. It was time, and I was more than ready.

Breaking away from the kiss, I stared deep into his eyes. His face was flushed and his eyes were dark with desire. I'd never seen him look more beautiful.

"I want you to top me," I said.

He gasped, eyes growing impossibly wide. He opened his mouth, but no sounds came out.

"I... you... Pardon?" he managed to stammer after a while. "Alpha... how... never!"

I chuckled at his reaction. "I want you, Eban. In all ways. This is one way we can have."

"But..." he started before giving up.

"It's a simple solution. I can't take you because it takes your magic, but there is no reason you can't take me."

He stared at me, looking so incredulous that it made me laugh.

"Only if you want to," I clarified. "It's fine if that's not your thing at all."

He swallowed audibly. "Gosh, I've... I've never even considered it before and... alphas don't..."

I gave him a quick peck on the cheek. "Alphas do whatever they hell they like."

He grinned at that. His gray eyes so bright they flashed silver. I ran my hand tenderly down his back.

"It's incredibly romantic of you to offer, but I don't think it would work."

I frowned at him but waited for him to explain.

"The conventional wisdom is that the act of submitting and being subjugated is what forces a vessel's body to give up their magic. But I have come to suspect that it's more the effect of having an orgasm. Hard for your mind and body to hold on to its magic in the throes of an orgasm."

I mulled over his words. They made a lot of sense. I knew in the moments of rushing through my peak I would be unable to hold on to any part of myself. It explained why giving him a blowjob had caused him to spill some of his magic along with his seed.

"But what if you bottom for someone and don't come?" I asked.

I didn't like the suggestion that Hyde was a good lover and always satisfied Eban. It didn't fit the image I had painted of their relationship.

Eban blushed. "After the first time, a vessel's magic learns that sex brings it freedom, so it always drives the body to its peak. Vessels always come."

I stared at him. People said the exact same thing about omegas. It was used as an excuse to treat them awfully. 'Omegas always spill when given cock.' Therefore they must love it and want it. Always. From everyone and anyone at any time.

Anger rolled through me, leaving me trembling. Then another thought struck that increased my anger into a rage. If Eban was right, it meant Hyde could drop to his knees and pleasure Eban and take his magic that way. But instead mages had created a culture where vessels were made to surrender their bodies, even if they didn't want to. A culture where they were treated as lesser. Subservient to mages. It was so unfair.

It also meant something horrendous. Something my mind tried to balk at.

"I can't ever give you an orgasm?" I exclaimed in horror.

He shrugged. "But I can give you as many as you can handle."

My inner wolf perked up at that and wanted to focus fully on that point. But I shook my head angrily to clear it.

"I couldn't spill, knowing you can't," I protested even though it was probably a lie. I was an alpha in my prime. Spilling my seed was something I was very good at.

"Pleasuring myself seems to be fine. Maybe you could watch?" Eban said. Then he shyly bit his bottom lip. I loved seeing his shy side, it was adorable.

His words sunk into my soul and ignited my arousal. It burned all other thoughts from my mind. The only thing existing in my head was the thought of watching Eban stroking himself to completion.

"Yes please. Now please," I croaked incoherently.

He chuckled and rolled onto his back. I threw off the covers, so that I could see everything clearly. He watched me with heavy-lidded eyes as his long elegant fingers wrapped around his hard cock. I sucked in a breath.

His hand danced lightly up and down. Wordlessly, I reached for the bedside cabinet where I had placed a bottle of lube. Snapping the lid open and holding it up high, I poured it over his cock and his hand without touching him. He took in a shaky breath and continued to glide his hand up and down. Smearing the lube everywhere until his cock was glistening.

"Slower," I rasped.

He quirked an eyebrow at me, but did as I bid. Slowing his strokes right down. I licked my lips. I wanted to savor every last second of this.

"When you get to the top, run your thumb over your slit," I ordered.

Again, he did as he was told. He gasped as he did so and I grinned. I was going to control his every single movement, and make him give himself the most wonderfully torturous handjob in existence. I was going to eek out his pleasure until he was a sobbing, pleading mess.

"Tighten your grip," I instructed.

His breath quickened, and his cock swelled. Mine throbbed almost painfully. Watching him was one of the hottest things I'd ever seen. In reality, not being able to touch Eban was awful but thankfully the kinky part of my brain was able to fire up and enjoy the whole forbidden thing. I could look but I could not touch. Might as well make it fun.

His head tilted backwards as he moaned, inadvertently baring his long slender neck to me. My lips itched to descend upon his skin, the thought of pressing my teeth into him made my wolf want to howl with need.

Eban's paced quickened and his eyes closed.

"I didn't say you could speed up," I said.

Obediently he slowed again, giving a little whimper of frustration that warmed my belly.

"Open your eyes and look at me."

His beautiful eyes fluttered open. He held my gaze but flushed and squirmed.

"Good boy," I breathed happily.

The wail that escaped him was beautiful. He liked my praise, and I liked that a lot. My hand found my own cock and started stroking in time with his movements.

"No!" he panted. "I want to suck you off."

I pulled my hand away. Even without touching myself, I was fairly certain watching Eban was going to make me come. But I'd try to hold out. I liked a challenge, and I liked the thought of his lips around my cock even more. I groaned.

"Play with your nipples," I said.

His free hand rose to one pink already swollen nub. He pinched it and moaned, his eyes nearly closing again. But he opened them before I had to tell him to.

He twisted his nipple again, and his whole body squirmed. He was sensitive there. One day I'd lick and nibble him until he begged me to stop. I'd sit behind him, pull him close to my chest and torment both his nipples at once, while he writhed in my lap.

Pre-come dripped out of my cock. A sudden urge to let Eban spill so I could blow my load too, nearly won me over. But I resisted. All good things come to those who wait.

I toyed with the idea of getting him to finger himself. The mere thought made me groan out loud.

"Stop," I told him.

He stopped immediately, but kept his hand wrapped around the base of his cock. He stared at me imploringly, eyes fever bright and his hips making tiny thrusting movements.

"When I say go, you are going to stroke yourself as fast as you can and you are not going to stop until I say so."

Eban frantically nodded his understanding. I leaned closer until the distance between us was tantalizing.

"Keep your eyes open and don't look away," I said.

He nodded.

"Go," I whispered.

He must have been desperate to come, because as soon as I gave permission, his hand flew up and down his cock. He cried out and his back arched off of the bed. His hips spasmed, but his eyes never left mine.

The intensity of his gaze as he orgasmed blew me away. I saw the pleasure in his eyes. I saw him overwhelmed by lust. I watched as all his walls came tumbling down and I got to see into the brightness of his soul. I felt my own walls crumbling in return and knew he could see all of me. Down to the very core of my being.

"Stop," I gasped.

He lay there panting. His cheeks flushed red. Looking all sweaty and spent and utterly divine.

"That was hot," he breathed.

I could only nod. There were no words for what I had just experienced. The intimacy that I had felt.

"Is your magic okay?" I asked eventually. I hadn't touched him, so in theory it should be no different from sorting himself out in the shower. But if I knew one thing about magic, it was that it was fickle.

He nodded happily before giving me an evil grin. The gleam in his eyes stole any thoughts I might have had about being relieved that his magic was untouched.

"Now lie down and let me suck your cock," he said imperiously.

I lay down on my back so fast I made myself a little dizzy.

"I won't last long," I warned. Probably only to the moment his lips touched me, if truth be told.

"Oh darling, you wouldn't last long with me at any time," he promised sweetly.

I groaned in anticipation. It was turning out to be an excellent night.

Chapter Twenty

Hyde gave his permission for Eban to visit his friends without quibble. A fact that mildly surprised me. It made me wonder if the man was trying to make amends or if he simply had no use for Eban for a couple of days and therefore didn't care. Whatever the reason, we were free to go, and I was strangely excited about it.

I packed my bags in a few moments and then sat in a chair in Eban's rooms and watched him be a complete diva. The poor staff were scurrying around trying to pack things to his exacting specifications. The mountain of suitcases that started to form, was alarming me. It looked like supplies for an army for a month. Not the things one person needed for a weekend in a country house.

Just as I was about to voice my concerns, Eban declared that everything was now packed and should be taken to the car. I had visions of sitting amongst piles of suitcases in the back of the limo. So, I watched with dismay as the staff efficiently carried the luggage away.

Eban smiled at me, and we made our way to the waiting car. Miraculously, the back seats were empty, though I did spot some suitcases piled up on the front seat by the driver.

I held the door open for Eban and then climbed in after him. As soon as I shut the door, Eban pressed the button to raise the privacy glass between us and the driver. Then he slid over to me with a wide grin. My heart skipped a beat as my mind caught up with what was about to happen.

Four hours alone with Eban in the backseat of a limo. No interruptions, no intrusions, complete privacy. I grinned.

Wrapping my hand in his long silky hair, I pulled his head up to just the right angle. Then I kissed him. Deeply, desperately, intensely, while I pushed him down onto the seat until he was lying on it and I was over him.

It was a very fun journey. We fooled around like horny teenagers and then when we were finally tired of that, we talked about our favorite films. Then most precious of all, Eban curled up next to me, rested his head on my shoulder and fell asleep.

As the car pulled up in front of a large country estate, a wave of disappointment washed over me. More intense than any I'd ever felt in my life. The house was lovely, but it meant the journey was over.

Eban woke up, yawned and smiled warmly at me. He didn't seem to mind that our precious time together had ended. Trying not to feel too disgruntled I climbed out of the car and held the door open for him.

Eban bounded up the stairs to the front door where the butler was waiting. I trailed after him. He was shown into a light and airy parlor. The four men sitting in it drinking tea, rose politely when Eban entered. One was Charlie but I did not recognize the others.

"Oh Eban, I am so delighted you could make it!" gushed Charlie.

The tall man beside him had dark curly hair and blue eyes. He shook Eban's hand and gestured to the incredibly handsome man standing next to him.

"This is Lord Garrington, oh heavens, I mean Mr. Montfort."

Mr. Montfort grimaced a little but said nothing. Eban shook his hand and gave him a dazzling smile.

"I've already had the pleasure," Eban said brightly, hinting at great familiarity.

Charlie squeaked and covered his mouth with his hand.

"Not like that," drawled Eban seductively. "Sadly," he added with a wink.

The beautiful young man with striking silver hair standing next to Mr. Montfort stared at Eban in alarm.

"Don't mind Lord du Fray, he is always like this," said Mr. Montfort gruffly.

Eban laughed, sounding like he wasn't at all offended.

Mr. Montfort gestured at the silver-haired man standing next to him. "This is Fen, my boyfriend and my vessel, so kindly desist from flirting with me all weekend."

Eban sighed dramatically. "I can't flirt with Hathbury," he gestured at the man who had started the introductions, "and I can't flirt with you. What on earth am I going to do all weekend?"

Before anyone could respond to that, Eban turned slightly, grabbed my arm and pulled me forward so I was standing next to him instead of behind him.

"This is Bastion, my lover," he declared.

Four pairs of eyes stared at me as I fought not to blush under the sudden scrutiny.

"I told you!" hissed Charlie to Hathbury.

Silence stretched for an awkwardly long time. Then Hathbury was shaking my hand.

"Ah well, jolly nice to meet you, please call me Archie."

Mr. Montfort offered his hand next. "Xander," he said. Then his eyes narrowed. "Wolf shifter?"

"Problem?" I challenged in a low voice.

"Ugh!" said Eban as he stepped between us. "Play nice you two. Xander may be the human equivalent of an alpha, but he isn't actually one. No need for a pissing contest to prove dominance."

"I was merely curious," stated Xander, looking me straight in the eye so I could see the honesty in his words. I nodded back at him and just like that the tension dissipated.

Except Fen was now staring at me, his bright blue eyes impossibly wide and his face pale. Xander took his hand and gave it a little squeeze.

I stared back at Fen, and he flushed. "Oh, I'm sorry! I was raised by mundanes. I've never met a werewolf before."

Charlie coughed. "The polite term is wolf shifter."

Fen clamped his hand over his mouth, his eyes filling with horrified dismay. "Gosh, I'm sorry. I didn't know." He whacked Xander on the arm. "He never tells me anything."

I chuckled. "It's fine."

Fen only looked slightly less mortified, but it was a start.

"Have a seat!" said Archie brightly. "Let me pour you some tea."

A footman hurried forward with a chair for me and just like that I was sitting with nobles and drinking tea with them as an equal. I had no idea what Eban was thinking. I simply had to have faith that he trusted these people and knew no word would get back to Hyde.

I sipped my tea and listened to the polite small talk. Sitting next to Eban instead of standing behind him was nice. Being introduced as his lover had made me feel all warm and tingly inside. Spending the whole weekend openly with him and not having to hide anything, was going to be wonderful. I felt a grin spread across my face and couldn't stop it.

Chapter Twenty-One

Eban had said he was going for a swim over an hour ago, but I suspected he was still there. The smell of chlorine led me to the outdoor pool hidden on the grounds.

Eban was indeed still swimming laps. I was glad to see he had decided to wear trunks, instead of swimming naked like he usually did. They were very tiny, very short trunks, but it was the thought that counted. It was completely irrational but the thought of anyone else seeing him naked filled me with rage.

He saw me and stopped by the edge of the pool.

"Hi," he said with a warm smile.

"Hi," I repeated.

I stared at him mutely for a moment. He was so very gorgeous. It was tempting to change my plans and jump into the water with him.

"Will you be alright for a bit? I thought I'd go for a run, since we are out in the country," I finally managed to say.

He blinked up at me for a moment then his eyes widened. "As a wolf?"

I nodded, feeling strangely apprehensive. Knowing abstractly that I was a shifter was one thing. Me saying I was about to run around as a wolf was quite another.

"Can I see you? In your wolf form?" he asked.

I stared at him.

"Unless it's private or something…" he started to say but I interrupted him.

"I'd be happy to show you, if you are sure?"

He nodded, gray eyes gleaming in excitement and curiosity. He really did want to see me and that knowledge flipped my heart over.

Carefully, I stripped my clothes off and folded them neatly. Leaving them in a tidy pile on the grass. Giving Eban one last glance, I closed my eyes and let my wolf surge free. The shift took mere seconds.

Opening my eyes, I saw Eban staring at me in wonderment.

"Oh my, you are beautiful," he gasped. "So unfair! Why do you get to be ridiculously good looking in two forms?"

I padded up to him, ignoring the sting of the chlorine in my nose.

"Can I touch you?" he asked.

I lowered my head so he could reach me. He raised a hand out of the water and gently brushed his fingers along my ruff. My fur was too thick to feel the wetness but I wouldn't care anyway.

"Fen should be here to see this, he is fan boying over you so hard."

I huffed. This moment was for Eban only. It was for us, no one else.

Eban laughed, "I really am banging a wolf shifter!"

He pulled his hand back under the water. The air was nippy and the water was heated so I wasn't offended.

"They have some magic thing to explain to me at lunch. Something they have discovered about what vessels can do. It will probably bore you to tears, so take your time with your wolfy stuff."

I wagged my tail at him, turned around and sped off. Happiness filled my entire being. I was going to spend the next few hours running in the woods. My paws on the earth and all the delicious smells and delightful sounds of nature washing over me. Then when I was done, I was going to come back to Eban. Life was perfect.

Several hours later, I trotted back to the swimming pool. Someone had put my clothes in a plastic bag, which was great as it had rained a little while I had been running.

I sniffed the bag. Eban's scent was all over it and no one else's. He hadn't thought of it and ordered a servant to do it, which would have been sweet enough. He had taken the time to do it himself. My heart fluttered crazily in my chest.

Shifting swiftly, I threw on my clothes and jogged up to the house. I found Eban in the bedchamber we had been given for our stay. He was standing and staring pensively out of the latticed window. I snuck up behind him and wrapped my arms around his waist and rested my chin on his shoulder. He flinched at first and then melted into the embrace.

"How was lunch?" I asked.

"Great. Very informative."

I waited to see if he wanted to tell me more.

"They have discovered that vessels are far more powerful than we are led to believe."

Somehow, I wasn't surprised. People and societies throughout the world and down through history had contorted themselves to subjugate those with power. How humans treated women was a prime example.

"Anything that will help you get free of Hyde?"

He shook his head. "No."

I hid my disappointment. It had been foolish to hope that our problems would melt away so easily. Nothing was going to change in a hurry. I needed to accept that. It was the price I needed to pay to be with Eban.

"Is there time to ravish you before dinner?" I asked.

He laughed. "Maybe."

I scooped him up and carried him over to the bed where I deposited him gently. He looked up at me and grinned.

"What did you have in mind?"

I gave him my best naughty smirk. "I'm going to eat your ass and hold you on the edge of orgasm for hours. Then I might let you finish yourself off."

His eyes grew huge and his mouth fell open. I chuckled as arousal swirled low and urgent in my belly.

"I think you like the sound of that," I rumbled.

He flushed and nodded. Then he started whipping off his clothes. I laughed again in sheer delight. Eban was going to love having my tongue in his ass. I was willing to bet good money that nobody had ever pleasured him like that before. I was going to give him the introduction of his life.

He was going to be writhing, moaning and whimpering underneath me in no time. He was going to pant and gasp and cry out his pleasure. His hips were going to buck helplessly until he was begging for me to let him come.

It was going to be wonderful.

Chapter Twenty-Two

I heaved myself out of the pool, grabbed the fluffy robe and scrambled into it as quickly as possible. It was freezing out of the water.

My gaze fell to Bastion's clothes folded neatly on the grass. Gray clouds were rolling lazily across the sky. It was going to rain.

I had stuffed a plastic bag in the pocket of my robe. Wearing wet trunks was the worst, so my plan had been to take them off as soon as I was finished, and bring them back into the house in the bag.

Walking around one's host's house in nothing but a robe was not too heinous a crime. I'd be going straight to my room anyway.

But I couldn't let Bastion come back to wet clothes. So I kneeled on the grass and carefully tucked his things into the plastic bag. Then I made the uncomfortable walk back in cold soggy trunks.

A quick shower to wash the chlorine off and then it was time for lunch. I stared at the clothes I had brought with me, looking for something that wasn't flashy or sexy but not scruffy either.

It was a challenge, my shopping choices had always been based on ways to flaunt my body. I didn't want to do that today. When packing I had been in denial about how I would feel. Sighing in defeat I pulled up some plain jeans and a tee shirt. Items I had packed with the intention of wearing only in my room.

There were two mages here, and I had slept with both of them. Hathbury had told Charlie at some point, I could see it in the vessel's eyes. It was testament to how sweet Charlie was that he still wanted to be my friend.

I'd never met Xander's boyfriend before. The look of dismay in his eyes at my flirtatious greeting to Xander had stabbed me with guilt and caused me to backpedal. I hadn't missed the flash of gratitude in Xander's eyes.

It was all ancient history and long before either of them had met their loves. But emotions were rarely logical. Like my own. Bastion knew what I was, but the thought of him knowing about Hathbury and Xander filled me with dread. A thought that stupidly hadn't crossed my mind when I had first opened my mouth to greet Xander. Thank heaven's Fen's pained look had brought me to my senses.

Bastion would never know about Hathbury and Xander.

Both had been only once and both at Hyde's behest but I still didn't want Bastion to be confronted with what a whore I was. Knowing I was one, was one thing. Meeting men I had been with was quite another. Hopefully, he would never know. Guilt at the deception snaked through me. Angrily I shook it away. It was a miracle Bastion liked me at all. I would not do a thing to risk that.

Neither man was going to say anything, I was confident of that. Our secrets were safe. Both were good men, I suddenly realized. My seduction of Hathbury had been cruel. But Xander had asked for me, having liked what he had seen. I'd been insulted and dismayed when he had never asked for me again. Pleasing mages was the one thing I was good at. Thinking that I may have been losing my touch had thrown me into a panic.

But now I understood he wanted more than obedience from his partners. He wanted them to enjoy it too. It had not been a rejection. It was him being a decent person.

I made my way to the dining room. Charlie greeted me with a big smile, the others acknowledged me politely.

"Is Bastion not joining us?" asked Hathbury.

"I thought magic talk would bore him, so I suggested he went on a run instead," I said. "As a wolf," I added when I failed to get the reaction I was hoping for.

Fen stared at me, his eyes wide as saucers. I grinned in delight. That was more like it.

I took my seat and tucked into my lunch. Images of Bastion in his wolf form filling my mind. He was stunning. A person of wild unfettered magic. A child of the moon and the wild. My thoughts turned to Bastion in his human form. Fierce, loyal, proud. Kind, gentle, caring.

I really did not know what he saw in me. Magic and looks were the only things I had going for me. He wasn't interested in the magic and I didn't think my looks were enough on their own to hold anyone's attention. It wasn't like I had much of a personality.

I dragged the spoon through my soup morosely. He was going to tire of me soon enough. Hastily I blinked back tears. Borrowing pain from the future was futile. It was important to enjoy the present. I needed to savor every precious moment with Bastion.

"We have some interesting information about vessels to tell you," said Hathbury, startling me from my thoughts.

I looked up and waited for him to continue.

"It seems magic can be transferred without intercourse."

I'd figured out about orgasms being the key by myself, so this wasn't a tremendous revelation.

"And vessels can call back all the magic they have previously given."

My eyebrow raised at that one. It was a lot to take in. It changed the fundamental pillars of everything I had ever been taught about mages and vessels.

"Xander and Fen are experimenting and it seems likely we are going to discover even more."

This was dangerous knowledge. It had the power to change everything. People would kill to keep this all a secret and maintain the status quo.

"Why are you telling me?" I asked and winced at how much my voice shook.

To my surprise, it was Charlie who answered. "We are hoping you can use it to get free from your husband."

I blinked at him. "What? You think I can suck my magic out of Hyde and be allowed to waltz off into the sunset?"

It was a ridiculous idea. There were far too many powerful people whose best interest would be to stop me from getting away with it. They wouldn't want their own vessels getting ideas.

I stared at them all incredulously and got nothing but sheepish looks in return. Two mage and vessel pairs who had found love and were able to be together. Did they have any idea of how lucky they were? Most people could only dream of what they had. Dream of it and know they would never have it.

"Excuse me," I murmured as I scrambled to my feet, the chair scraping behind me.

The others rose politely to their feet too, but I didn't acknowledge them. I just fled to my room. The knowledge that I could never have what they had, heavy in my gut. Even if he was stupid enough to want me, Bastion would never be mine.

And if that wasn't miserable enough, an unmistakable tingle in my belly told me I was going to be ripe soon. Probably tomorrow. It was all too much to bear.

Chapter Twenty-Three

Eban was quiet on the journey back. I sat beside him and worried if last night had been too much. I had pleasured him with my tongue for hours, until he was a sobbing pleading mess. He had cried out and clenched around me, making me think I had gone too far and tipped him over into his orgasm. I had scooted off the bed, making sure no part of me was touching him. He flopped over onto his back, stroked himself three times and came gloriously. I watched from the floor, stroking myself. We came more or less together. Mere seconds apart but what felt like miles in distance.

The sight of him lying flushed, sweaty and boneless on the bed would stay with me forever.

"Is your magic okay?" I had panted.

He nodded weakly, and I had climbed back into bed with him. All had seemed well.

But now, looking at him staring forlornly out of the car window, I wasn't so sure.

"Are you okay?" I asked.

He turned to me with a sad smile. "Yes. I'm just not thrilled to be going home."

I took his hand and gave it a squeeze. That was perfectly understandable and mirrored my own feelings. I was relieved it wasn't anything I had done. It was good to know that I hadn't pushed him too far. Sex was complicated for him. I didn't want to overwhelm him or make him feel vulnerable.

The journey back to London was long, yet not long enough. I yearned to recreate the joyous feel of our trip up to Hathbury House but Eban's somber mood permeated the car.

It was late into the evening when we pulled up in Mayfair. We had left late, putting it off for as long as possible. Then we had hit horrendous traffic on the motorway.

Eban flowed out of the car as soon as the driver opened the door. A flurry of staff appeared to whisk all the bags back to his rooms. I left them to their work and followed after Eban. I was confident the staff could identify which bag was mine, and deliver it to the right place.

Eban went straight to his rooms. He stood there, radiating tension and misery whilst the staff bustled around him. It was like he was a brooding island in a sea of movement.

Hyde walked in and my heart sank. No doubt he was going to berate Eban for being late.

"You are ripe," he snapped.

My stomach clenched as everything suddenly made horrifying sense. This was why Eban was upset and distant. It hurt that he hadn't told me.

"How observant of you, dearest husband," quipped Eban.

Hyde frowned. "You're early," he growled, before rounding on me. "Did you fuck him?"

I opened my mouth to reply but Eban beat me to it.

"No, he didn't. Check my memories if you must. The well of magic that Hathbury House is built on is strong, and I soaked it up. That is all that happened."

Hyde glared at him for a moment. Then he strode towards Eban's bedchamber and flung the door open.

Eban sighed heavily. "May I unpack and have a bath first?"

Hyde's jaw clenched. "Fine. I'll return in an hour."

I watched Hyde storm away and clenched my fists. My wolf wanted to rip his throat out and taste his blood. I took several deep shaky breaths.

"What can I do to help?" I asked Eban.

He gave me a weak smile that did not reach his eyes. My arms ached to hold him but I didn't know if that was what he needed from me right now.

"In the nicest possible way," said Eban. "I'd like to be left alone."

I nodded my understanding, gave him a smile and shuffled away to my room. I sat on my bed in a daze. Hyde was going to take Eban's magic. He was going to fuck him. I'd promised I wouldn't run away again. I needed to be here when it was over, so I could comfort him. Which meant, I had to stay in my room. Where I would hear and smell everything.

My fingers dug into the mattress. My lungs burned, and I realized I had forgotten to breathe. I sucked in a breath. The challenge ahead seemed impossible. In my darkest depth of my soul I could not devise a worse torture. I was an alpha shifter, Eban was mine, yet I had to sit passively, helplessly, while another man touched him, abused him.

The deep ominous growl that echoed around the room startled me. It had escaped from my throat. I needed to get a grip. I had to stay in control. The man I loved was about to be hurt. He was going to need me afterwards.

I sat there in a daze. Listening as Eban had a bath. I heard him move around his bedchamber, then get into bed. Hyde came into his room. I winced and closed my eyes.

Breathe in, breathe out. Stare at the cobweb high on the wall. Breath. Hold on to the mattress.

The sound of Eban's bed creaking as Hyde moved onto it assaulted my ears. I whined and tightened my grip on my bed. I started to count to one hundred. I could do this.

I thought of fleeing to another part of the house, but no part was far away enough. Nowhere in the world was.

Breathe. Count. Hold on to the mattress. It was fine. I could cope.

Eban whimpered.

I burst through the door. Hyde jumped up from Eban's bed. I growled deeply, only realizing as I did so that I had shifted to my wolf form. I didn't care. The mage was going to die.

My nose told me that nothing had happened yet, and as much as that satisfied me, I was more focussed on keeping it that way.

Hyde summoned magic and created a ball of orange fire in the palm of his hand. It felt like Eban. Because it was formed of all the magic Hyde had stolen from him over the years.

I snarled and stepped forward. He could throw his puny little ball of magic at me, it wasn't going to stop me sinking my teeth into his throat. Suddenly Eban was between me and my prey.

"Stop it! The pair of you!" he snapped angrily.

He was wearing a long white nightgown that was pretty much see through. He placed his hands on his hips.

"I suppose I should be flattered that a mage and a shifter are fighting over me, but frankly it's ridiculous."

He had been extremely brave to step in between us. But a large part of me wished that he hadn't. I was confident I could destroy Hyde.

My human side argued that it wouldn't solve our problems. It babbled about other mages and consequences. But Hyde was the only enemy in front of me now. I could deal with any others later.

Eban sighed. "Hyde, I suggest you let Bastion do the honors. I suspect if you stay in my living room, you will be close enough to draw my magic to you once he has loosened it."

Hyde gave Eban a skeptical look but I could tell he was intrigued.

"If I'm right and it works," continued Eban. "You can write a paper on it and everyone will think you are frightfully clever. If I'm wrong..." he trailed off and shrugged. "Well, I'll be ripe again soon enough."

Hyde stared at him.

Eban glared back. "It's better than you two having a death match!"

Hyde's gaze flicked back to me. I felt my hackles raise and another rumbling growl eased out of my throat.

"You both want different things!" said Eban urgently.

He turned to Hyde. "You want my magic. He wants me. You don't need to fight over anything. You can both get what you want."

Hyde gave him a long intense look. "Fine, only because it is an interesting experiment. Otherwise I'd be putting the mut down."

I stifled my growl. Eban was working hard to stop everyone killing each other, and it was working. Hyde was agreeing not to touch him. I wasn't going to jeopardize that. On the very slim possibility that Hyde could defeat me and then hurt Eban after I was dead. The tiny part of my mind that was still rational reluctantly acknowledged that a shifter defeating a mage was not a bet I'd place money on.

Hyde strode out of Eban's bedchamber, closing the door sharply behind him. Just like that Eban and I were alone. I shifted to my naked human form and stared at him. Suddenly feeling the weight of what I had just done.

"Sorry," I breathed sheepishly.

He shook his head and held out his arms. "Come here."

I was wrapped around him in seconds. Holding him close to me and breathing in his divine scent. Hardly daring to believe he was here and safe.

"Make love to me," he whispered.

I scooped him up and carried him to his bed. As I lay him down, I stared deep into his eyes.

"Bare your throat to me," I begged.

His eyes flashed silver. "What exactly would I be agreeing to? What does it symbolize?"

I adored how clever he was. I took in a deep breath. "That you are mine."

He smiled and tipped up his head. No hesitation. No fear. No doubt. My teeth descended onto his throat, pressing in lightly. Not enough to break the skin. I whimpered in delight. He gave a little moan of satisfaction.

The taste of him was exquisite, and I'd longed to do this since the very moment I had lain eyes upon him. Finally he was mine. Eban was mine and it was everything I needed.

Chapter Twenty-Four

It wasn't a mating mark, but it was a start. Eban had submitted to me and accepted me as his Alpha. He was mine to protect. My pack. My everything.

It was far more than I had ever hoped for. My lips kissed their way up to his and I feasted on him. The way he melted into my kiss was food for my soul. I deepened the kiss, and he moaned beautifully, his whole body raising off the bed to meet mine.

With a growl, I broke away. Only to rip his nightgown off in one determined move. He gasped as his eyes flashed silver. The horrid leather thing on its gold chain was lying on his chest. I picked it up, giving him a questioning look. I didn't want him to need it with me. He nodded his consent, and I whipped it over his head, throwing it on the floor with disgust. Then I attacked his mouth again.

I was going to make love to Eban. Fully. Finally. No pulling away and having to let him orgasm alone. No need to hold back and control myself. Just free unfettered passion. It felt too good to be true. A privilege I did not deserve. Yet, that was obscene. It should always be like this between us. Love should not be confined and Eban should not belong to another man. He should be free to choose. Like he had chosen to bare his throat to me.

His hands wrapped around my neck as his tongue explored my mouth. He was hungry and eager and it was divine. It pushed all thoughts and worries from my mind until the only thing that existed was this moment and him.

The scent of him combined with the fragrance of his arousal washed over me. The heat from his body seeped into me. My hands ran over his smooth skin. His soft sounds of pleasure filled my ears and the sight of his bright gray eyes brimming with lust burned into my soul. He overwhelmed all my senses. I was aware of nothing but him. He was everywhere and everything and I drank it all down like a man dying of thirst.

His sounds turned needy. He was ripe. He needed me. My hand drifted down to between his legs. His hole was oiled and opened. Gently I slipped a finger inside of him. He cried out, his hands clutching my shoulders. Lost in pleasure. I added a second finger to check he was ready for me, I didn't want to hurt him. I wanted him to feel nothing but pleasure.

I slid in knuckle deep. He groaned as his legs spread wider and his hips lifted up, chasing my touch, asking for more. He wanted me inside him. The knowledge left me awestruck and humbled. It was a privilege I was proud to have earned.

Reluctantly, I withdrew my fingers so I could get into position over him. I looked down into his eyes to check he was ready. His cheeks were pink, his eyes hazy with desire. Nothing but longing and anticipation in their depths.

Slowly, carefully, I started to give him my cock. Easing inside of him gently. Spreading him, stretching him, filling him. His tight heat took me well, welcoming me. Enveloping my hard cock with bliss.

He threw his head back and cried out. A sound of satisfaction and euphoria. I sunk all the way into him. Then stilled, gasping and panting. All my nerve endings firing in ecstasy. Waiting until I was sure he had adjusted to my size.

Then I flipped us over so I was lying on my back and he was sitting above me, straddling me. He gave a little yelp of surprise then stared down at me in sheer astonishment. I had suspected that he had never been allowed to do this. Seeing the confirmation in his eyes caused a flare of anger. I ignored it. He was doing it now, with me, and that was all that mattered.

My hands grabbed his hips and I lifted him up and down. Sliding him up and down my cock. He groaned, his eyes fluttering closed. I guided him with my hands for a few more thrusts until he got the hang of the movement. He learned quickly as I knew he would. He moved gracefully in all that he did.

As soon as I was sure he had figured out how to ride, I let my hands fall away. Letting him set the pace and rhythm. Giving him control. I watched him move above me, taking his pleasure. It was the most incredible sight I had ever seen.

My cock swelled and I groaned. I was in heaven. Eban picked up the pace. His hands rested on my chest to give him more leverage. His head tipped right back, exposing his long slender throat to me.

His cock was full, bouncing enticingly along with his movements. Pre-cum leaking steadily out of the tip. I wrapped my hand around it and started caressing it. Eban cried out, shuddered and clenched delightfully around me. The sensation tore a groan from me. My knot started to form. I grunted in dismay. Eban was human, he couldn't take my knot.

I put my hands back on his hips and flipped us over again, so he was lying on his back. Using every inch of self-control I possessed, I pulled my cock out. Eban whimpered in dismay but I swiftly slid back in, but this time it was not all the way. I couldn't put the base of my cock, where the knot was forming, inside him. I could still give several inches and it still felt damn incredible for me but there was an edge of frustration.

He was moaning beautifully now. Writhing and undulating beneath me. Riding the waves of pleasure I was giving him. He was close, very close. I debated on whether to drive him to his orgasm with just my cock or if I should stroke him too and give him dual delights. Then an image flashed in my mind of him playing with himself and how sensitive his nipples were.

I bent my head, bowed my back and rasped my tongue along his nipple. He squealed and bucked. I set to licking, sucking and nibbling. Moving my weight onto one hand, I used my now spare hand to toy with his neglected nipple. He screamed, clenching so tightly around me it stole my breath away.

I did not stop nor slow. My hips thrust my cock in and out of him in the same rhythm. I continued to suck on one nipple while rubbing the other between finger and thumb.

His orgasm rolled throughout his body. His muscles spasmed. A low gurgling groan hissed out of his throat. His ass convulsed around my cock and warm wetness spurted between us where his cock was trapped.

I kept going and so did he, the wave of his peak riding high and long before finally cresting. He gave one last shuddering gasp before going completely limp. I looked down at him in alarm. His eyes were closed, his face slack. His limbs sprawled bonelessly on the bed.

I pulled out of him.

"Eban?"

Nothing. No response at all.

"Hyde! Hyde!" I bellowed.

He was only next door. He would hear me. Sure enough, the door opened and he walked in.

"He's out cold! What's wrong?" I demanded.

I twisted my neck to look over my shoulder at Hyde. His dark gaze flicked to Eban and then back to me.

"It's fine. It happens. Their magic leaving them can be intense for vessels."

I swore and turned my attention back to Eban, wiping some stray strands of hair back from his face.

"Don't you need to check?" I asked.

"No," said Hyde arrogantly.

The knowledge that Eban had been this vulnerable with Hyde, ignited a dark deep rage that settled low within me, where I knew it would smolder for eternity.

I gritted my teeth. "Did it work?"

Knowing if Hyde had taken his magic might help me figure out if Hyde was right and there was nothing to worry about. Or if I needed to ignore him and get someone else to help.

"Yes," said Hyde. "Very well. I gained more magic than usual."

I turned my head to look back at him. I had not expected him to say that.

Hyde looked thoughtful. "It is said the more a vessel enjoys themselves, the more they give up."

I'd never wanted to punch anyone in the face more, but Eban was out cold and naked in my arms. I wasn't leaving him.

Somehow I wasn't surprised that treating vessels well benefited everyone, but mages still preferred to be cruel assholes. Choosing fear and subjugation over increased magic. Vile monsters. However, there was a silver lining.

"So we can do it this way from now on?" I growled at Hyde. Eban's clever plan had worked far better than expected. There was no reason for Hyde to touch him ever again. Eban could truly be mine. I could protect him.

Hyde narrowed his eyes. "He is my property. Bought and paid for."

"He is a person! Not a slave!" I bellowed in outrage.

"I will consider it," said Hyde coldly and with a haughty tilt of his chin he strode away.

I was glad to see the back of him. Now I could just focus on Eban. Lying down beside him, I pulled him into a spoon. His breathing was even and regular. His heartbeat sounded good. It irked me to trust Hyde, but I had little choice. I held Eban in my arms and waited for him to wake up.

Chapter Twenty-Five

Eban woke with a start thirteen minutes after Hyde left. He tried to scramble up, every muscle in his body tense, but I tightened my arms around him.

"Hey, I've got you. Everything is okay," I soothed.

He collapsed back into my embrace with a relieved sigh. I nuzzled his neck.

"Did it work?" he asked.

"Yes," I confirmed. There was no need for him to hear the rest of it.

He wriggled around to face me. His eyes still looked a little unfocused but his color was good. He smiled at me.

"That was incredible," he breathed, sounding awestruck. Then he blushed a beautiful shade of red.

I pulled him close and tucked his head against my chest. Stroking his hair.

"Thank you," I teased.

Pressed against my chest, he chuckled warmly.

His hand drifted up my chest to my shoulder and down my arm. Then suddenly his fingers dug into my bicep as if he was clinging onto me.

"Stay," he pleaded softly.

"Of course," I rumbled and kissed the top of his head.

I didn't know if he meant the night or forever, but he was getting both.

The next day Eban had a funeral to attend. Hyde didn't bother to come. A fact that lowered my opinion of him even more. Accompanying your husband to a family funeral was basic politeness. It was testament to just how much Hyde didn't care. He couldn't even be bothered to pretend it was a proper marriage.

It was Eban's elderly aunt who had passed away and all the guests appeared to be treating it far more as a social event than an outpouring of grief and mourning. The ceremony was brief, but the wake was lavish. Mage society was really starting to grate on me.

I frowned as Eban took yet another glass of champagne from a passing server. It was frustrating being his bodyguard and not his lover. There was nothing I could say or do to try to gently dissuade him from drinking too much.

He was chatting exuberantly to a couple I did not recognize. I stood behind him. Ignored. Invisible. Just his bodyguard.

A whip thin man in his late fifties, with slicked back gray hair approached. The moment Eban saw him he flinched and stepped back towards me until he was nearly standing on my toes.

"Mr. Richards, what a pleasure to see you," Eban purred.

The man inclined his head politely. "Lord du Fray."

"I wasn't aware you knew Lady Somerset?" asked Eban.

His voice was even and calm but Eban was close enough that I could see he was trembling. The scent of his fear burned in my nose and made my wolf snarl. Who the fuck was this Mr. Richards and what had he done to Eban? He looked so unassuming.

"The Earl and Countess invited me, it seems they have rethought their modern ways and are considering formal training for young master Witherington," said Mr. Richards.

"Colby?" gasped Eban weakly.

Mr. Richards nodded. "They have come to realize it will make him far more desirable on the marriage market."

"I see," said Eban.

An awkward silence stretched.

"Please excuse me," murmured Eban.

Mr. Richards bowed his head politely, and Eban fled. I followed close behind him. He wove through the crowd, straight to the toilets where he sat in the furthest cubicle, put his head in his hands and sobbed.

I fell to my knees in front of him. Luckily the floor was gleaming and spotless. Not that I would have cared.

"Hey, what's wrong? Who the hell was that?"

"My trainer," Eban sniffed.

He glanced up at me with teary eyes and saw my confusion.

"There is a lot of ritual and formality to being a vessel. Ways to be quiet and biddable. Named positions to assume."

I stared at him in growing horror. Positions to assume? For sex? Was that what he meant?

"And that man taught you?"

Eban nodded.

"How old were you?"

"Sixteen."

I hadn't realized I had got to my feet until I felt Eban tugging on my arm.

"Darling, as wonderful as watching you rip out Mr. Richards' throat would be, it won't change a thing."

I stared back at him doubtfully. The creep being dead would change a lot of things. It would feel damn good too.

"It was not that bad," said Eban. "I was technically a virgin for Hyde."

"Bastion!" Eban called sharply as he chased after me.

I stopped in my tracks, halfway to the door. I hadn't intended on moving. I took a deep shuddering breath. It did nothing to calm me.

"We need to help Colby, not worry about ancient history."

I growled. Killing Mr. Richards would solve that problem too. Killing Hyde would be wonderful. A groomed, virgin, eighteen-year-old Eban had been delivered to Hyde's bed. No one involved deserved to live.

I'd seen Eban tremble. I could still smell his fear. He was downplaying it. Making light of it because he thought it didn't matter. Eban thought he didn't matter. I needed to teach him that he did. He mattered more than anything in the world.

Eban made an exasperated noise. "Dating a possessive, protective, stud sounds so swoony. In real life it's a pain in the ass!"

I turned around to face him. "Sorry."

He smiled fondly at me. "It is still swoony and the sex is mind-blowing."

We stared at each other. I longed to embrace him but anyone could walk in. Eban was right in front of me, yet so far away. It was torture.

"Now calm down and help me think of a way to save Colby," he said.

The only person I wanted to save was Eban. There had to be a way to take him far away from here, but so far the solution had eluded me.

The chances that I could devise a cunning plan to save Colby were slim to none.

"We have to get him a proposal from a mage who doesn't care about training," said Eban.

It was a great idea, but I had no idea how to achieve it. The mages' world of scheming and plotting was beyond me. Wolves were far more straightforward.

"He likes Rakewell, I'll go talk to him," beamed Eban. "This is a splendid plan. Thank you!"

He darted out of the bathroom. Dazedly, I turned on my heels and followed. I wasn't sure why he was thanking me. I'd merely stood there gormlessly as he had thought out loud, but I was happy if it had helped in any way.

Eban made a beeline for the duke, seeming to find him as effortlessly as a homing pigeon finds home.

"Your grace!" gushed Eban. "It's been an absolute age since I have had the pleasure of your company!"

The duke had been standing alone, admiring a portrait on the wall. He turned to face Eban with an expression that could only be described as terrified. I could sympathize. Eban was like a force of nature.

"Lord du Fray," he nearly stuttered in greeting.

The duke looked to be around Eban's age. Handsome in the typical tall and dark-haired way. He wasn't broad but there was definitely a hint of muscle. My guess was that he regularly enjoyed some sort of sport. I could see why Colby had his eye on him. The kid had good taste at least.

Eban launched into small talk. The duke answered politely but falteringly until Eban's conversation unearthed Rakewell's passion for polo. Then the young man came alive, his eyes sparkling.

Eban was excellent at this. I listened in awe. Eban seemed to be knowledgeable about polo but the more I listened, the more I realized he only had a rudimentary understanding. But he used it to guide the conversation and encourage it. Mostly he appeared to hang on Rakewell's every word. Listening in rapt attention.

He inched in closer and started touching the duke's arm as he laughed at his words. It was hard not to bristle. I didn't know what he was up to, but I trusted him. Eban leaned in close to Rakewell.

"It's awfully stuffy in here. Do you fancy joining me on the balcony for some fresh air?" whispered Eban seductively.

The duke flushed a deep red right to the roots of his hair. "No thank you," he said sternly with a flash of affronted anger in his eyes.

Eban laughed, "Perfect! Sorry to tease you, your grace." Then he turned to me. "Would you be a dear and find Colby for me?"

Nodding smartly, I went on my way. As I left, I heard Eban continue his conversation.

"I adore my cousin. Colby is such a sweet young man. I'm going to give him a modest allowance to support his polo playing endeavors, once he is married, because I'd hate to see him have to give it up."

Keeping my chuckle to myself, I wove through the crowd. I found Colby by the buffet.

"Excuse me Mr. Witherington, Lord du Fray would like to introduce you to Duke Rakeswell."

Colby looked up at me with big brown eyes.

"Oh," he gasped. "Oh!"

He hurriedly put his plate down on the table and pulled his jacket down. Before smoothing his shirt with jerky nervous movements.

"Oh gosh, do I have food on my face?"

I smiled, "No, you look great."

He beamed at me, and I led the way.

"You love polo," I whispered when we were halfway there.

"Pardon?" he exclaimed in alarm, glancing up at me with a worried look. Then his eyes lit up. "Oh! I see. Thank you!" His smile was dazzling.

He seemed like a lovely kid. Daft, but lovely. Rakeswell seemed decent too. They would be a good match. I hoped Eban could work his cunning charm and get it to happen. Keeping Colby out of Mr. Richards' hands would be satisfying.

Chapter Twenty-Six

It was raining heavily when it was time to leave the funeral. Bastion held a large black umbrella over us both as we waited at the top of the steps for the car. I hadn't seen where he had got it from. But the fact he had warmed my heart.

In truth, it was what any decent bodyguard would do, there was no reason to feel soppy about it. I shouldn't treat the gesture like it was attentive and showed he cared. However, everything Bastion did made me want to swoon. My foolish mind determined to twist it into some romantic fantasy.

Bastion was wonderful. In every way. I knew that part to be true. Thinking he could possibly love me was ridiculous. It had to be just a fling for him. He knew me. Knew me better than anyone else on earth did. He had seen into my very soul. There was no way he could like what he had seen.

I was vain, shallow and insipid. It was a miracle he hadn't run a mile. I was going to treasure and worship every moment I was granted with him. He was the most amazing person I'd ever met. It was a privilege to be in his presence, let alone have a fling with him. I knew I would cherish our time together till the end of my days. I'd never meet anyone who could hold a candle to him.

I stole a discreet glance up at him. He was the love of my life. No doubt about that. The knowledge made my heart thump. Soon we'd be alone in the back of a car together. I hoped he would kiss me. Hold me. I wanted to close my eyes and pretend it was forever.

A car pulled up but it wasn't ours. I sighed in impatience then winced. I didn't want to remind Bastion that I was a spoiled brat. I wanted him to think better of me. As futile as that was. But for some reason, I still wanted to try. At least he had seemed pleased by my desire to help Colby.

I wasn't convinced that made me a good person. Anyone would want to help the innocent fool. Colby was a naïve idiot. An over excited puppy that didn't deserve to be shown the darkness of the world. Helping him was satisfying, and it appeared to be going well. Duke Rakewell had voiced several modern opinions and refused my advances. He was a good man, as far as I could tell.

Colby had done a great job at pretending to be polo mad. The deception felt a bit mean, but Colby was lovely, if exceedingly annoying. Rakewell couldn't hope for a better vessel. He just needed a bit of help in seeing that.

Raised voices caught my attention. Some mundanes had stopped on the pavement by one end of the U shaped drive and were arguing. A beefy looking man and a tiny woman with long red hair. He slapped her hard and she staggered back against the wall.

Bastion thrust the umbrella into my hand and ran down the drive. My heart swelled. He was so chivalrous.

Suddenly, cruel hands were digging into my arms. The umbrella tumbled down the steps. Two huge men all but picked me up and bundled me into the car that had pulled up earlier. I was too shocked to do anything but squeak. Somehow Bastion heard me, he turned his head, paled and started sprinting back towards me.

The car sped off with a squeal of tires. I twisted around on the back seat so I could look out of the back window. Bastion was in the middle of the road, running after me with supernatural speed. He was about fifteen feet behind and somehow gaining ground. Could shifters run faster than cars? It looked like I was about to find out.

He looked hotter than hell, pounding down the road in his dark suit. His jacket flapping behind him and a grim, resolute expression on his face. He didn't look like a bodyguard running after his charge. He looked like a man running after his lover. Desperate. Furious. Utterly determined. It was the most swoon worthy sight I had ever seen.

I whimpered in dismay at myself. I was being abducted by lord knew who, for heavens knew what, and the only thoughts in my head were dirty ones about my bodyguard lover.

One of the kidnappers sitting beside me swore and rolled down the window. My mind was working like treacle and I didn't move until he leaned out.

"No!" I gasped as I desperately grabbed the brute and tried to haul him back in. His friend pulled me back, and the gunshot rang in my ears.

Red bloomed on the white shirt covering Bastion's stomach. I screamed, but he didn't even falter let alone slow his pace. The gun fired again, and I saw Bastion tumble to the ground before the car took a sharp turn and he was out of sight.

I screamed in horror and attacked my abductors. Hitting, scratching, kicking, but I was no match for them and they soon had me overpowered. One holding my arms behind my back, the other holding my legs. I wriggled stupidly before slumping in surrender.

Angrily I blinked back tears. I didn't want these assholes to see me crying. But the image of Bastion falling to the floor played over and over in my mind in startling, horrifying clarity. I tried to bite back my sob, but it escaped me and soon I was weeping and wailing inconsolably. My shoulders and chest heaving until I started hiccuping.

The only silver lining was that my crying seemed to make the goons holding me far more uncomfortable than my pathetic attempt at fighting them had. Good. I'd cry forever if it unsettled them. It wasn't like I was ever going to be able to stop anyway. I couldn't care less what they did to me, the only thing I cared about was Bastion.

I prayed he was alive. I prayed everything I had ever heard about shifter healing was true. I'd give my life for his in a heartbeat. Sell my soul to a demon. Anything. He had to be okay, he had to be.

I couldn't have caused the death of the only man I would ever love.

Chapter Twenty-Seven

"Eban!" I yelled as I finally fought my way to consciousness.

"Shh," said someone as they firmly pushed me back down onto the bed.

I opened bleary eyes.

"Colby?" I croaked in confusion.

He nodded distractedly, his attention was fixed on my abdomen and, judging by the smell, the herb poultice he was pressing against it.

My gaze flicked to Denise standing stoically by the door, resolutely staring into the middle distance. She was good at being unobtrusive. I didn't mind her presence. Colby was an unmarried vessel. He couldn't be alone with anyone or a scandal would be caused.

"How long, where?" I demanded.

Colby sighed. "You've been out for three hours and fifteen minutes. You are in one of the guest rooms in the house where the wake was held. I saved your life. You're welcome, now stay still before you undo all my hard work."

"You're a healer?"

He flushed and nodded. "I'll give it up when I'm married of course, but for now it keeps me occupied."

I looked down at my stomach, half expecting to see gaping wounds. Colby removed the poultice to reveal two large, very pink scars. He had done brilliantly.

"Thank you," I gasped.

He beamed at me.

"My phone?" I pleaded.

Colby frowned a little but reached over to the bedside table and handed me my phone. I snatched it and called Hyde. He answered on the second ring.

It had to be about money. Hyde was obscenely wealthy. It was the logical conclusion. Moon help me if the mage had done something idiotic like piss the mob off and it was personal, not financial.

"Has the ransom demand come through," I snapped before he could say anything.

"Yes," he bit coldly.

A dizzying wave of relief washed over me. "Great. Where and when is the drop off?"

"I'm not paying."

"What?" I breathed in incredulous horror.

"I don't negotiate with criminals," he declared haughtily. "I could buy two new vessels with what they are asking for."

"You... you can't just leave him!"

"The fault is not mine. You were supposed to be his bodyguard. Seems I have no more use of you. You're fired."

The line went dead. I stared at my phone blankly. My mind refusing to accept what I had just heard. I knew the mage was an asshole, but this was a whole new level. Surely no one in the world could be so heartless.

"What a bastard!" declared Colby, his brown eyes blazing furiously.

I jumped, I had forgotten he was there. In my addled state, I'd put my phone on speakerphone. Our eyes met. I had one ally at least. What on earth was I going to do?

"I don't suppose you have any inside info?" I asked.

He gave a startled look. "I do thrive on gossip, but I haven't heard that Hyde was in a feud with anyone."

"It could be mundanes? Targeting him because he is rich?" I suggested.

Colby shook his head. "The car was an exclusive model that is only sold to Old Blood."

It took me a second to remember that Old Blood was what mages called themselves. This was great information. Ruling out all the mundanes in the world narrowed the field down considerably.

"Who amongst the Old Blood is having money problems?" I asked.

His eyes widened before turning thoughtful. He tapped his finger against his lips in a gesture that was extremely endearing.

"He hasn't got the balls. She is too dumb to plan something like this," he said as he thought out loud.

I waited with bated breath as he pondered.

"Lord Buckingham, Lord Farney or Duke Cartingham," he announced proudly.

None of those names meant anything to me. I huffed in frustration. Colby fished his phone out of his pocket.

"Wait a minute, let me find some pictures of them. You can see if any of them have been lurking around suspiciously."

I nodded despite my dismay. It was worth a try. Even though I was certain no one had been lurking around suspiciously. I would have noticed that. I wasn't usually a terrible bodyguard.

Colby held up his phone. A picture of an old man in a blue suit glared back at me. I'd never seen him before in my life. I shook my head.

Colby fiddled with his phone for a little while before holding it up again. This time it was a chubby middle-aged man standing awkwardly in the doorway of a fancy house. Again I shook my head.

Colby found the next picture quickly and showed me. A jolt like electricity ran through me. It was the man who had cornered Eban in the bathroom at the dinner party. Hyde had punished Eban for it but maybe he also had words with the duke and disgruntled him. The duke certainly hadn't looked pleased at my interruption. Add in money problems and it was the perfect recipe.

"Duke Cartingham?" asked Colby, clearly reading my expression.

I nodded mutely. A suspect was a great start. But it was only a start.

"Any ideas where he would keep Eban?"

Colby looked thoughtful again. "He owns a hotel in Camden?"

A hotel was perfect. No one would bat an eyelid at strange people coming and going. Keep a few rooms empty by the room you were using and no one would hear anything, but even if they did, most would discount it as normal arguments that were often overheard when staying in a hotel. It was nothing like suddenly hearing your neighbors at home being violent out of the blue.

The location was perfect too. Camden was a busy part of London and only a few miles away. They wouldn't have had to transport Eban very far.

"Colby, you are a genius! I could kiss you!"

He flushed bright red. "I don't think Eban would approve."

I laughed. Eban was going to be alive and well to disapprove. I was going to rescue him and he was going to be safe.

"Can I get up?"

Colby frowned. "Shifters heal ridiculously fast but not that fast, give it another hour at least."

I growled in frustration. Eban needed me. I couldn't just lie here. My heart raced and my wolf snarled. They won't be hurting him, I tried to tell myself. They just want money. There was no reason to harm him. My wolf wasn't listening.

"Let's use the time to work out our plan," said Colby.

"Our?" I questioned, raising an eyebrow.

"That's right, our," he said with a stubborn set to his chin.

I sighed in defeat, I was going to need all the help I could get.

Eban's other friends were over four hours away. There was no way on earth I was going to wait that long to get Eban back.

Chapter Twenty-Eight

Five minutes before my hour was up, I fired a text to Hyde, as I couldn't bear to talk to the man. I told him the plan and invited him to provide backup. If he could get Eban back for free he might help, but I wasn't going to hold my breath.

The precise second the hour was up, I jumped out of my sick bed. Wincing as my insides pulled, but I continued dressing in the garish clothes that Colby had somehow rustled up for me. He gave me a worried look but said nothing. Presumably he could see that I was not going to wait any longer.

I turned to Denise. "Are you okay with this?"

"Hell yeah," she said, lifting up her jacket and tapping her gun fondly.

I liked her even more. Rescuing Eban was far from her job description as Colby's bodyguard. She didn't need to agree to come along and help. She didn't even know Eban. Either she was an incredibly good person or she liked a fight. Whatever the reason I was happy to have her.

The three of us made our way to the front of the house where a car was waiting. Heavens knew what Colby had told his parents, but they were nowhere in sight.

It was only a couple of miles to the hotel but two miles in central London took an age in early evening traffic. We should have walked, it would have been quicker. I drummed my fingers against my thigh impatiently for the whole journey.

Finally, we arrived at the very nondescript hotel. As per the plan, Denise stayed in the car. Colby shot me a look that was both nervous and excited. I gave him an encouraging nod. He was being very brave in getting involved with all of this.

I wrapped my arm around his waist and staggered into the lobby. We wove our way up to reception. It was early to be drunk but not notably so. Camden was a lively part of London.

Two men in dark suits were doing a terrible job at looking like they were just hanging out in the lobby. They watched us suspiciously. I pretended not to notice them at all.

I felt naked without my sunglasses but not having them was part of my disguise. Luckily people rarely truly noticed bodyguards. Out of our suits and glasses and not in our customary place in our employer's shadow, we were rarely recognized. I was banking a great deal on that right now.

I grinned at the receptionist as if I didn't have a care in the world.

"I'd like a room please," I slurred.

"Do you have a reservation, Sir?"

I pulled Colby closer to me. "Nope. I wasn't planning on getting lucky."

Colby giggled and flushed. I wasn't sure if he was acting or not.

The receptionist stared at us. Drunk. No luggage. No reservation. Attempting to check in at a strange time. My blatant comment. She frowned, and I held my breath, half expecting her to declare that this wasn't that sort of hotel. Our simple plan could fall down like a house of cards.

Trying to check in any other way, would have looked too suspicious. This way we looked naughty, but should not catch the interest of the men in the lobby. But if the receptionist was going to be prudish, we were done for.

"Do you have a problem with us being gay?" asked Colby indigently, placing his hand on his hip.

The receptionist flushed. "Not at all."

I mused how everyone, even homophobes hated being accused of being homophobic.

She typed quickly onto her computer, took my cash and swiftly issued me a keycard. Colby was a genius. His quick thinking and great acting skills had saved the day. She was so determined to prove that she wasn't a bigot, she didn't ask any further questions.

I discreetly glanced over at the henchmen lurking in the lobby and saw with relief that they had lost interest in us. Our plan was working. Two drunk gay guys hooking up in Camden was believable.

Fumbling, I fetched my phone out of my pocket and pretended to just be checking it briefly, while I sent Denise a blank text. I dropped it back in my pocket and swayed over to the elevators whilst still holding Colby.

Denise walked through the lobby nonchalantly while excluding a calm air of belonging. She joined us at the elevators but we pretended not to know each other. I slipped the keycard into the slot to unlock the call bell.

The doors opened with a soft ping a few moments later and we filed in. I entered the keycard again to select a floor. Opting for the top one. As soon as the doors shut, Colby made to step away from me but I tightened my grip on him and gestured with my eyes at the CCTV camera. He caught on quickly and went back to leaning against me.

As soon as the doors opened, I knew we had figured it out correctly. Eban's tantalizing scent drifted down the corridor. Top floor had been a good educated guess. The most defensible and had no neighbors above to hear anything. The room on the furthest corner was my best bet and as we ambled down the hallway, my nose confirmed it.

I glanced around. There was no one but us. I wondered if anyone was watching us on the CCTV, I could only pray that they weren't. Hopefully, our act in the lobby and in the elevator had fooled anyone watching and they weren't suspicious of us and were no longer watching. If they were, and came to ask us why we were on the wrong floor, an excuse of being too drunk to know which floor we were supposed to be on would buy us some time, but not enough.

The best course of action was to act quickly. I let go of Colby and plastered myself against the wall, gesturing to Colby which door Eban was behind. Denise lined up behind me and we were as ready as we would ever be.

Colby took a deep breath and knocked on the door.

"Henry! I lost my key! Let me in. I'm drunk and I'm sorry, forgive me!" he wailed convincingly.

I heard footsteps inside the room. They approached the door but made no further movement. They were hoping Colby would go away.

I gave Colby a 'carry on' look.

"Please Henry! I love you! I want you! You are the only one for me!" he yelled while hammering on the door.

I heard faint swearing from inside the room. With any luck, they would now be looking out of the peephole and seeing a very unthreatening looking twink.

The door unlocked. "You've got the wrong room, kid."

Right on cue, Colby dived aside so Denise and I could storm in. There were only three guards. Between the element of surprise, my shifter strength and Denise's gun, it took seconds to overpower them.

Denise hustled them into the bathroom and locked them in. I ran over to the bed where Eban was sitting. He looked unharmed. His wonderful hair was damp and curling and he was dressed in fresh clothes. They had let him take a shower.

I threw my arms around him. "Are you okay?"

"I'm fine," he assured. "Nothing but bored."

Though the way he was clinging onto me hinted he wasn't as unfazed as he was making out. I held him tightly. Joy surging within me at the feel of his body against my own. He was here. He was safe. It was incredible.

Thundering footsteps on the hallway pulled my attention away. The plan for getting out of the hotel was the weakest part. Hinging mostly on luck and finding a fire escape. I swore and spun around to face the door, keeping Eban firmly behind me. My wolf snarled and growled, ready for anything.

Several armed men burst in. They were Hyde's. Relief flashed bittersweet. I knew what was going to happen next. Sure enough Hyde strode in. Giving me only the briefest of disdainful glances. His men took Eban away from me and hurried him out of the room.

Eban went without resistance. Without even looking back at me. But I could smell his dismay. I knew how devastated he was. My wolf whined in confusion. Hyde could get Eban safely out of the hotel but it meant he was taking Eban away forever.

"You're still fired," snapped Hyde, turning on his heels and striding away. Surprising no one with his words.

I sagged on the bed in defeat. All of my fighting spirit suddenly knocked out of me. I had rescued Eban from his abductors but had only succeeded in returning him to his vile husband. It didn't feel like there was much point in anything anymore.

"Come on," said Colby, pulling at my arm. "We still need to get out of here before Cartingham's reinforcements arrive."

I stared at his worried brown eyes. I needed to get him to safety. I owed him that much at least. Hauling myself to my feet, I leaped into action. Once Colby was out of danger, then I could collapse into a heap of misery. Until then I had work to do.

Chapter Twenty-Nine

I stared out of the car window. Trying to hold on to the feel of Bastion's arms around me, but it was fading like a ghost, and I didn't know if I would ever see him again. But I almost didn't care. He was alive, and well enough to rescue me. That knowledge brought me nothing but intense joy.

Those five hours of not knowing if he was amongst the living had easily been the longest of my life. Seeing him had been wonderful. A moment of pure divine bliss. Even if it was to be the last time.

I wasn't at all surprised that Hyde had fired him. It was always only ever going to be a matter of time. Bastion being unable to stop me from being abducted was a perfect reason.

It wasn't all bad. He was better off without me. If he was away from me, I couldn't fuck up his life or get him killed. It was for the best. I finally understood the 'if you love someone, let them go,' saying. I loved Bastion and that meant I wanted the best for him. I wasn't the best. He could have a long and happy life without me.

I would yearn for him forever, but knowing he was well, was enough. It would have to be.

London fell away as the car purred along the motorway. I realized Hyde was taking me back to the country estate, not the new house in Mayfair. It was a shame, I loved London. The lights, the vibrancy, the life. I was going to miss it.

Hyde sat silent and still beside me. After a while he took out his phone and started making business calls. As if everything was well and his husband hadn't just been abducted. It was fine by me. I didn't want to talk to him either. There was nothing to say.

I knew Hyde was furious. He didn't give a shit about me as a person. But the fact that someone had dared to steal his property and made him look weak would enrage him. It was a small mercy that he wasn't taking it out on me. Hopefully, he would focus his energy on getting revenge on Cartingham. If he didn't just report him to the Council. The crime of stealing a vessel carried the death penalty.

I continued to stare out of the window until exhaustion from the stress of the day and the gentle movement of the car lulled me to sleep. I didn't dream of a thing. It was almost peaceful.

It was nearly dawn when the crunch of gravel woke me up. I blinked up at my country home. It was a lovely house but it was a gilded cage. Far more than the Mayfair house. There was nothing out here for miles. No distractions. No escape. Nothing but my own company.

The footman opened the door, and I climbed out of the car. Striding straight to my rooms without looking back at Hyde. The familiar surroundings engulfed me. The staff had done a good job at looking after the place well. There wasn't a speck of dust or any musty smell. It was like I had been away mere moments instead of months.

Except everything had changed. Last time I had been here, I hadn't met Bastion. I'd never seen his kind smile or heard his deep laugh. Never felt the softness of his kisses. I was someone new now. Irrevocably changed, and my whole life now defined by two distinct periods. Before Bastion and after Bastion.

Numbly I selected some pajamas from the chest of drawers, grateful that both houses were always kept fully stocked of everything I might need. I quickly changed into them, deciding against a shower. I had just had one a few hours ago, before being rescued and all I had done since then was sit in a car. My soft bed was calling me and I longed to sink into it and forget everything for a while.

Hyde stalked into my room. I didn't turn around to face him. Staring blankly out of the window instead.

"Are you damaged?" he asked.

Damaged. Not hurt or even injured. Damaged like the property I was.

"No."

"Did Cartingham fuck you?"

I sucked in a breath, unable to stop myself. "Yes. After you refused to pay the ransom."

A slight pause before he answered with, "Do you need the healer?"

Was he trying to be nice? Was that his attempt at making amends? It was pitiable if it was.

"No," I snapped, probably far sharper than I should have.

I felt him bristle behind me, felt his mood darken but it was too late to do anything about it now.

"I assume you have washed him off of you?" growled Hyde.

I grimaced, hating that he would have seen my shoulders flinch. I didn't want my husband to have any part of me. I didn't even want him to know his words affected me.

"Yes," I answered with gritted teeth.

"Good. Get on the bed."

Shock and horror filled me. I whirled to face him as I fought a ridiculous sense of disbelief. There was nothing wrong with my hearing. He really had ordered that. But why? His dark eyes glinted. Anger and frustration swirling in their depths along with wounded pride.

My own anger answered. "You want to stake your claim? Mark your property like an animal pissing on what is theirs?"

Color flushed along his cheeks, and his eyes narrowed. My heart beat frantically as adrenaline surged throughout my body.

"You dare to talk to me like that?" he snarled. "I have always been far too lenient with you, no more!"

I backed away, just one step. My subconscious screaming at me to get away from the danger. But my rational self knew running away would merely enrage him further. And he had spoken the truth. He was lenient with me. I was often flippant to him, giving him the barest level of respect a vessel was supposed to give their master. I was often sarcastic and cheeky. Nevermind all my indiscretions. Even though Bastion had given me a lightbulb moment and shown me that they may not be my fault, I still felt guilty. Dirty.

He glared at me. "I will have your obedience. I will have your submission. You will behave as a vessel should. Meek. Respectful. Biddable."

Some part of me spoke before the sane part could stop myself. "And taking me to bed will do that?"

He stepped towards me. "Yes," he said darkly. "I have finally learnt how much you hate laying down for me. I will use it to break you."

I couldn't move, couldn't breathe. Couldn't even think. All my thoughts had come screeching to a halt.

"Get on the bed!"

He grabbed my shoulders and threw me onto the bed. Then he yanked my pajama trousers down. I stared up at him, frozen. He had expressed remorse after the hospital incident. Why was he doing such a u-turn? Was he blaming me for being abducted?

He undid his belt and fly, then his dark eyes met mine. Full of anger, rage and insult. His words rang in my ears, 'you hate lying down for me,' he had said. Comprehension dawned. He thought I despised sex with him but gleefully sought it from others. That belief had been festering and now had come to a head.

He was a powerful, dangerous man, and I had made him feel lesser. Inadvertently demeaning his manhood. Added to the fact I'd been abducted, an event that declared to the world that he was weak enough to be challenged, and I was in a world of trouble. He was going to take all his rage out on me.

Maybe before Bastion I could have borne it. But not now. Not after Bastion had taught me how it should be. Now the very thought made my skin crawl and my stomach heave in revulsion. Hyde had reached breaking point but so had I. I couldn't take it anymore. It would destroy me and I didn't want to be destroyed. I wanted Bastion. My soul called for him. It demanded to survive, so the hope that I'd one day be back in Bastion's arms could live.

My hand slid under the pillow, the feel of cold metal sent a jolt of relief through me. It was still there, where I had left it months ago. I whipped the dagger out and held it against his throat.

He froze. Shock widening the whites of his eyes. We stared at each other, both motionless. Our rapid breaths the only sound in the room. What now? Despite everything I didn't want to murder him. But if I released him, it would all be over. Hyde would beat me savagely and then keep me chained to a bed for the rest of my days.

Lightening fast, I flipped the dagger over and smacked the handle against his temple. He collapsed on top of me like a sack of bricks.

Grunting, I heaved him off of me. I pulled up my pajama trousers, shoved my feet into the pair of slippers waiting by the bed and ran.

Chapter Thirty

Walking down the road in the pouring rain while wearing pajamas and slippers was no fun at all. The morning sun had risen but it was still early and being in the middle of nowhere, there hadn't been a single car yet.

The village was three miles from the estate but I had decided to head in the opposite direction, towards the town that was ten miles away. Figuring that if anyone noticed I was gone, they'd search towards the village first.

My anxiety grew with every step I took. Sneaking out of the house had been easy, but surely any minute now Hyde would wake up and all hell was going to be set loose. Vessels were impossible to scry for, but I wasn't exactly going to be hard to find physically.

I was a vessel who had attacked their master, the consequences were going to be... My thoughts stuttered to a stop. I had no idea what the consequences were going to be. I'd never heard of a vessel doing such a thing. A shiver ran up my spine. The consequences were going to be bad, that was for sure. Society hinged on us knowing our place. They would make an example of me.

I wrapped my arms around myself and even though there was no one to see, I was still glad the rain hid my tears. The sound of an engine rumbled in the distance. My heart picked up pace and my first stupid thought was 'Bastion.'

There was no reason for him to be here, looking for me. He wasn't about to swoop in and save the day, and longing for my big burly lover to rescue me wasn't a very progressive thought at all. I was an adult, perfectly capable of saving myself. As nice as falling into his strong arms and letting him fix everything would be.

I sniffed. Thoughts and longing for Bastion filling my mind and soul. Maybe if I yearned hard enough, he would sense me? We were both paranormal beings, it wasn't entirely ridiculous.

I sighed. It was ridiculous, completely ridiculous. It was time to pull myself together.

I missed Bastion with all my heart and soul, and not just because I wanted to be saved like some princess in a tower. I missed his presence, his company. Everything about him. Even though we hadn't been apart for very long at all. His absence burned. But right now I needed to concentrate on surviving. Once I was somewhere safe I could think about finding Bastion.

The engine noise was closer now, coming up behind me. I whipped around. The country lane was winding and hilly and gave me a perfect view of the battered white van, even though it was still a fair distance away. I sighed in relief and continued trudging along. Just a local mundane. Hyde didn't own any vehicles like that.

The van reached me but instead of driving past, it stopped beside me. The driver rolled the window down.

"You alright, love? Do you need a lift?"

I stared back at the bearded, stocky man in his thirties. He had the deep sun kissed look of one who worked outdoors a lot.

"Oh sorry," he muttered, looking embarrassed. "I thought you were a girl."

I wasn't offended. It was probably the long hair or the pretty pajamas or my slender build. Okay, thinking about it, from behind I probably did look exactly like a girl. I wondered if he was going to drive off now he had realized his mistake.

His gaze tracked up and down my body. Probably taking in my bedraggled state. I couldn't imagine that I looked attractive at all, soaking wet and shivering. Hopefully, I looked such a mess that he wouldn't recognize me from opening the village fete or whatever.

"You want a lift, mate?"

Nodding gratefully, I yanked open the van door and climbed in. He fiddled with the blowers until hot air was wafting over me. Then he pulled away. I stared silently out of the window. Thankful for his kindness. My legs crying out in joy at being able to sit, and the hot air making me realize just how frozen I was. I felt guilty for dripping water all over his seat, but there wasn't much I could do about that.

"Thank you so much," I gushed, my voice trembling. "Are you heading into town?"

"Aye," he answered, keeping his eyes on the road. "I love your accent. Where are you from?"

I flushed. Tom Hiddleston managed to make Received Pronunciation sound hot when playing Loki in the Marvel films, but I was quite sure I just sounded like an idiot. Amongst my usual haunts, mixing with other nobility, it was fine. Everyone more or less sounded the same. Now I was out in the real world, it was going to stick out like a sore thumb.

"London," I mumbled sheepishly.

It was the best answer I could come up with. I couldn't exactly say I was from two miles up the road. Or that I had grown up in Devon. My accent didn't fit either place and claiming to be local would only invite more questions.

He turned to me and raised an eyebrow. "Posh London, not cockney London, I take it?"

I nodded in defeat. He flashed me a quick grin.

We drove in silence for a while. The heaters were doing a grand job of drying out my thin pajamas and the warmth was finally sinking into me. Maybe everything was going to be okay.

"Do you need money?" he asked.

I flushed again. I had been walking down the road in the middle of nowhere, wearing pajamas and slippers in the pouring rain at some ungodly time of morning. It was hardly a great leap of deduction.

I nodded mutely, unable to voice the words. Getting a lift into town was a fantastic start, but wandering around the streets in soggy nightwear would not be a great next step. I needed something to wear. A hotel room. Food. I had nothing but the clothes on my back.

"Want to earn some?" he asked quietly whilst keeping his eyes on the road.

My stomach flipped over, and my heart fluttered. Part dismay, part relief. I needed money, and this was familiar territory. I knew this. He might not be a mage or a rich businessman, and it was far more blatantly transactional than my usual endeavors. But at its core it was what my life had been for years. I could do this.

"What did you have in mind?" I asked sweetly.

He grinned again and pulled into a layby.

Chapter Thirty-One

The van driver dropped me off in the center of town. I jumped out of the van, clutching my cash in my hand as I didn't have any pockets. I gave him a wave, and he drove away.

Taking a deep breath, I set out to find a charity shop. I needed clothes, but I also needed my money to last as long as possible. It had been a pleasant surprise to discover how much a simple hand job was worth. Hyde must have been making a fortune out of me over the years.

As good as it was to know that my skills had value, it wasn't something I wanted to repeat anytime soon. I was running away in search of a new life, not to recreate my old one in shabbier surroundings.

I found a charity shop, just as it was opening for the day. The old lady unlocking the door gave me an odd look, but she said nothing. I found a huge black hoodie, a plain pair of jeans and a pair of ugly unbranded trainers that didn't look like they had ever been worn.

I decided to skip on a tee shirt, as well as underwear. The thought of second-hand underwear made me feel queasy, and I needed to save money.

The old lady pressed the buttons on the ancient till before asking for an amount that was half of what I had added up in my head. I glanced at her in surprise, were my math skills really that bad? Her kind brown eyes stared back at me kindly and steadily. I flushed and accepted her charity.

She let me change in the changing room and she gave me a plastic bag to put my pajamas in. I thanked her, probably too profusely and went on my way. Feeling infinitely better in warm, dry, discreet clothes.

My feet were really hurting by the time I had walked around long enough to find a cheap looking hotel. As I walked in, the receptionist glared at me. I felt myself wilt. I didn't look glamorous or rich. I looked poor and scruffy. Her reaction was something I was going to have to get used to, and it wasn't a pleasant feeling at all. Falteringly, I enquired how much a room cost. Her answer made my eyes water. Was she saying a ridiculous amount because she didn't want my custom or was it the real cost of things? I did not know. I knew nothing about the real world.

Dejectedly, I shuffled back onto the street. I was going to have to perform an awful lot of hand jobs every day to be able to afford to stay in a hotel. A cold wind picked up and blew right through me. What on earth was I going to do? How was I going to survive? And what the hell was I going to do when I became ripe? Everyone said only those with magic could empty a vessel and I had no reason to think they were lying. It meant if I didn't want to die, explode or go crazy, sooner or later I was going to need to find a friendly mage. One that would not turn me in.

That seemed insurmountable. But Bastion had been able to empty me. The thought flashed urgently across my mind. Finding a friendly shifter seemed far more plausible.

Find Bastion, whispered my soul. I closed my eyes against the power of that thought. It was probably a terrible idea. If by some miracle I found him, and was with him when I was hunted down, then Bastion would be charged with stealing a vessel. A crime punishable by death.

I needed to find somewhere safe to hole up first. Then I really needed to take my time in deciding whether or not to seek Bastion out. It was a momentous decision and one I couldn't make in a blind panic. I loved him. I wanted him. That meant I didn't want to get him killed. Or that he would even want to risk his life for me. On the other hand, it could be perfect. He might know a way to hide me away forever. He might want to. He might love me as nearly as much as I loved him.

I shook my head to clear it. It was too confusing and too emotional to think about right now. I needed to concentrate on finding somewhere to stay.

I walked around some more and then bought some food in a McDonald's. I had always heard that they were cheap, and I was greatly relieved to discover it was true. After that, the hours passed in a terrifying daze. The lonely world was nothing but a sea of cold concrete and crowds of strangers. I kept an anxious eye out for Hyde's men and Council enforcers. The whole thing was exhausting.

It started to get dark, and the horrifying realization struck me. I hadn't been able to find anywhere to stay. I was going to have to spend the night curled up in an alley without even a blanket. For a moment I wavered and considered going back to Hyde and begging for his mercy. If forgiveness was in his nature, I think I would have done it. But the knowledge that his retribution would be far worse than a freezing, terrifying night, kept me determined to see it out.

After peering down several alleys, I found a doorway halfway along one that looked dry and relatively sheltered. The door clearly had not been used for decades. I sat down on the cold concrete, placed my back against the bricks and curled up, resting my head on my knees. I was too tired to cry.

I must have dozed off because a gruff voice startled me.

"That's my spot,"

The man was grizzled and lanky. His clothes were filthy. I tried to scramble to my feet, but my bones protested and the best I could manage was a slow, stiff clamber.

"Sorry!" I told him.

To my surprise, he broke out into a wide toothless grin. "No worries, lad. There is room for two. Warmer that way."

He shuffled a large rucksack off of his back and started yanking out a grimy duvet. "Grab some cardboard from that bin over there and line the step."

I hesitated. "Um... do you want anything in return?"

He paused with the duvet half out of the bag and looked up at me. "Nah, lad. It doesn't work like that on the streets. You'll see. We all gotta look out for each other."

Nodding numbly, I scurried over to the large dumpster near the mouth of the alley and pulled out some large, flattened cardboard boxes. I was ashamed I hadn't thought of it for myself. Sitting on cardboard was going to be far warmer. Everyone knew that. I quickly covered the doorway floor with my find and sat down. The stranger sat beside me.

"There is room to lie down," he said.

I lay down. He tucked the duvet over both of us and spooned behind me. It was already far warmer and despite it only being a piece of cloth, having the duvet as a barrier between me and the world made me feel far safer.

"Sweet dreams," said my new friend.

I wasn't sure about that, but I knew I was going to sleep. And survive. The first day of the rest of my life.

Chapter Thirty-Two

Waking up shivering at dawn with a full bladder was a great start to my new life. Gingerly, I slid out from under the duvet. I didn't want to disturb my new friend or let any cold air in. I smiled in satisfaction when I stood beside him as he continued to snore softly.

Then I paced down the alley, looking furtively all around. I'd never pissed in public before. It was strangely unnerving. It took a bit of time to force myself to relax enough but I finally managed it. By then I was fully awake, and slipping back under the duvet felt weird. So I started wandering the streets instead. Moving to keep warm.

After sleeping on it, my cunning plan was to find the red-light district. As much as I hated the idea, I needed money. I didn't want to sleep rough forever. There were probably places like soup kitchens that gave out food for free, so I could possibly just about survive without any cash, but I wanted more than that. I wanted a home and a normal job. A nice life.

In the meantime, I had a skill set that didn't require a CV, an address or references. Perfect for my current set of circumstances. It would be foolish not to use them as a means to an end. Just until I was on my feet.

So, I'd find the red-light district. Hopefully, such things really existed and weren't a figment of Hollywood's imagination. Then I'd work it tonight. Unless there were pimps. The thought nearly stopped me in my tracks, with the terrifying knowledge that I did not know how anything worked.

Sighing morosely, I headed for McDonald's. I had enough money for breakfast, and it would be warm in there. Coffee would be fantastic. I'd deal with tonight, when it came.

I was sitting tucked away in the corner of McDonald's, sipping my coffee and wishing it was something stronger, when I noticed a man in a dark suit was watching me. My heart started racing. I didn't think I recognized him. I took another sip of my coffee and tried to sneak some quick glances his way to check. I was pretty sure I didn't know him, but that didn't mean I was safe. Hyde could well have told the Council about my crimes and enforcers could be after me.

Or I could be being paranoid. He could be completely innocent. He could simply like what he saw. With that thought in mind, I looked down at myself. My hood was up as far as it could go. My top was baggy and shapeless. It was already dirty. It seemed unlikely he fancied me. Unless he was drawn to desperate and vulnerable. In which case, he was another sort of threat.

My mood sank. That was just the sort of man I would be trying to attract tonight. It wasn't like I had the resources to dress up to appeal to any other type.

I grabbed my coffee and left. Suddenly convinced I would not survive the night. I didn't know what the hell I was doing. I didn't even know what the going rates were. I had a vague idea from the van driver, about the price of hand jobs, but for all I knew, he could have been being generous or the opposite and taking advantage of me. I had no clue about the value of any other services. Not that I wanted to offer anything else, but I realized that preference may be a luxury I could not afford.

The man was following me. That meant he had abandoned the meal he had barely started. The street was busy now, so I tried weaving through the crowd to lose him. Then I noticed a second man behind me but rapidly catching up. My heart started racing like crazy.

I picked up my pace, only to be confronted by two burly men striding towards me from the other direction. Panicking, I dove down a small side street, only to realize once I was half-way down it, that I was probably being herded, and I was going exactly where they wanted me to.

The small street opened up into a deserted car park. Empty apart from three glossy jet-black cars. I froze like a rabbit in the headlights. Several motorbikes roared up behind me, blocking my escape. I was done for.

"Eban," called a familiar voice. I whipped around convinced I was losing my mind. One biker had removed his helmet. My mind refused to believe that I was seeing Bastion. The man next to him also removed his helmet. The resemblance was striking. I looked at the biker gang. Bastion's pack. Bastion had brought his pack.

He had come for me. He wanted me. He cared enough to risk everything.

The sound of car doors opening behind me had me spinning back around. Hyde and several men, presumably enforcers, got out of the cars.

I heard growls behind me as the shifter pack faced off the men who had chased me to this spot. My mind slowly unraveled what was happening. Hyde had sent enforcers to hunt me down and Bastion had got his pack to hunt the hunters, in the hope of snatching me away from them.

"Eban, come with me," said Bastion.

I stood between the mages and the shifters and dithered. The temptation to run to Bastion was strong. I had never wanted anything more. But the mages would not let me ride off into the sunset. They would attack. The shifters and mages would fight. People would get hurt. People would quite possibly die.

I couldn't possibly do that to Bastion and his pack. They didn't even know me. I was nothing to them. The enforcers didn't know me either. They didn't deserve to die for doing their job.

I turned back to Bastion.

"No," I said. "I'm not worth it."

It would have been better if tears weren't streaming down my face, but I was powerless to stop them. I turned away from Bastion and ran towards Hyde.

"Eban!" called Bastion, and it sounded like a howl.

I reached Hyde, and he shoved me into one of the cars. The sound of fighting erupted. I wailed and covered my ears. What the hell was Bastion thinking? Why hadn't he taken his pack and fled? I was sure he had heard me. This wasn't what I wanted at all. Surrendering to Hyde was supposed to stop all this.

The fight raged on while I cowered in the back of the car. It was far worse than any nightmare I had ever had and there was no end in sight.

A horrid choking noise filled the air. I looked out of the window. Hyde had a cord of golden magic wrapped around Bastion's throat and was lifting him up into the air with it. Bastion's feet were dangling and kicking. His hands futilely trying to pull at the magic around his neck.

The other shifters were snarling on the floor. Each held down by a magic net wielded by an enforcer. They could not help Bastion.

I flew out of the car and yanked on Hyde's arm. "Let him go! You have me back!"

But Hyde ignored me. As immovable as rock. Two of the enforcers that weren't involved in the spell casting, hauled me off of him and held me between them.

Bastion's face turned red and then purple. He was dying. Hyde was killing him. Hyde would probably murder the entire pack. Because of me.

"No!" I wailed helplessly. Everyone ignored me.

I thought of Bastion's kind eyes. His rumbly laugh. His decency. His honor. He was a good man. Memories flashed of the feel of his arms around me. The feel of his kisses. The way he looked at me and actually saw me. I saw once again, him thrusting the umbrella at me before running without hesitation to help an unknown woman. Bastion didn't deserve to die.

Something within me snapped. "No!" I screamed in rage.

I felt Hyde's magic as it poured out of him to attack Bastion. So much of it had once been my own. Hathbury and the others had said vessels could call back their magic. So I gave it a go. I called it to me, and to my surprise, like a tsunami it came.

Hyde staggered, the magic around Bastion vanished. I didn't have time to see if he was okay. The enforcers holding onto me tightened their grip. I directed some of the magic that was pouring out of Hyde and back to me, towards them in an angry blast. They fell to the floor. Out cold. Somehow, I knew they were still alive.

Hyde fell to his knees. The euphoria of all my magic rushing back to me was overwhelming. I coaxed it to pour even faster. Hyde fell onto his back, gurgling in a parody of what he had been doing to Bastion. I strode over to loom over him. As the magic still rushed into me.

"Release me and I won't take it all," I said coldly.

He stared at me with beady eyes.

"Release me and I will leave you some of your magic. I will then go away and never be seen or heard of in society again."

He glared at me angrily.

"Don't release me and I will leave you as a broken husk and then tell all other vessels how to do this."

His eyes widened in horror, and he nodded sharply.

Excitement and glee bubbled through me. Tempered by fear. I wasn't sure I knew how to keep my end of the deal. I didn't know if I could stop what I started. I closed my eyes and concentrated. In the end, it was as straightforward as turning off a tap.

I opened my eyes and was pleased to see Hyde still gasping on the floor. He looked awfully pale.

"Tell them to let the shifters go," I ordered.

He nodded weakly, and I felt the magic of the nets dissipate. I heard the shifters get to their feet, but I kept my focus on Hyde.

"The enforcers can be the witnesses. Now do it," I commanded, enjoying my newfound power. I could get used to being a bossy bitch.

Hyde glanced up at me and then away, as if he couldn't bear my gaze.

"As my vessel, I release you," he said softly yet clearly. My heart thumped. "As my vessel, I release you. As my vessel, I release you."

Exuberance surged through me. He had said it three times. In front of witnesses. Officially, formally, in all the ways that mattered, I was no longer his vessel. He was no longer my master.

Bastion was on his feet, breathing heavily but otherwise looking delightfully unharmed. I ran up to him and threw myself into his arms. As his warm embrace enveloped me and he held onto me tightly, I completely destroyed my new bossy bad bitch image by bursting into hysterical tears.

It was over. I was free. I could be with Bastion forever.

Chapter Thirty-Three

Six months later

I walked through the pack house looking for Eban. The summer sunshine shone through the windows. The sound of his laughter drifted in from outside. I made my way to the back door and then just lurked there, staring at him.

'Mine,' said my wolf happily and being able to agree with him was the best feeling in the world.

Eban looked so beautiful it stole my breath away. He was sitting in the dirt, chatting to my brother's omega. My best guess was that they were weeding the vegetable patch, but I knew nothing about gardening, so they could have been doing anything.

Eban's glorious hair was up in a messy bun and held back by a red scarf. There was a smudge of dirt on his cheek and I couldn't wait to brush it off. He was wearing a pair of old battered jeans and a cheap tee shirt from Primark. I felt guilty that I couldn't buy him nice things or keep him in any way remotely resembling what he was used to. I had made an awful lot of money as a bodyguard, but it had all gone on buying more land for the pack and repairing the house.

He never complained. Instead, he was embarrassed by all the things he didn't know how to do. Like laundry or cooking or any sort of housework. Some things baffled me, like the fact he didn't know how supermarkets worked. I tried my best not to let it show, and focussed on teaching him. He was keen to learn everything. But gardening was definitely his favorite so far.

I stepped outside. Eban looked up at me. His gray eyes sparkled and he gave me a dazzling smile. His cheeks were tinged pink.

"Did you remember sun cream?" I exclaimed in alarm.

The time he had gotten sunburnt had horrified me. Humans were so unbelievably fragile. It was terrifying. There was so much I needed to protect him from.

He rolled his eyes at me. "Yes."

I stared at him for a moment, like the lovesick puppy I was. Then I remembered what I was supposed to be doing.

"This came for you," I said as I handed him the white envelope.

He wiped his hands on his jeans and took it. He opened it carefully and read it quickly. Then he looked up at me with a soft smile.

"I'm officially divorced."

Emma, my brother's omega, gave a cheer. I bent down and kissed the top of Eban's head. I was pleased it had come through so quickly. Then again, it wasn't surprising that Hyde didn't want to mess around. It pissed me off that he wasn't giving Eban a penny, but the wonderful thing was that Eban was finally free in every way.

"Do you know what this means?" he asked with a sly wink. "When you take me to bed tonight, it won't be adultery."

My cock twitched as arousal swirled low in my gut. Emma laughed, and I fought my blush, fairly certain that she had caught scent of my arousal. Hopefully Eban was oblivious.

He flowed to his feet. "I should put this somewhere safe."

I followed him inside and upstairs to our room. He placed the letter in a cabinet drawer. As he closed it, I snuck up behind him and wrapped my arms around his waist. He smelled amazing, all Eban and soil and sun. He leaned back into my embrace.

"No need to wait till tonight to try out this non-adultery thing," I rumbled.

He chuckled. "It's meeting night, I don't want to turn up all bow legged and exhausted."

"Are you saying I tire you out?" I teased as I kissed his neck.

"You know you do."

"Flatterer."

He turned around to face me and I stared deep into his eyes. Ever since coming home with me he had been softer, quieter. Subdued, with a haunted look that tore at my soul. So as always, I searched his gaze for signs he was happy. To reassure myself.

I grinned when I saw it. Eban was happy. His quietness was not my fault. It was still simply an effect of everything he had been through in his life. He had suffered so much and now he had been thrust into a strange new world with so much to learn. It wasn't at all surprising that he appeared a little subdued.

I leaned down and kissed him. Deeply, passionately. With all my heart and soul. He melted into it and by the time he broke away from it my cock was rock hard.

"Your meeting is not for hours," I whined.

He smirked at me. "But it is a special one. I will be getting a shiny one-hundred-day coin."

"Oh, Eban!" I exclaimed before devouring him hungrily again for several minutes. My hands caressing his body.

"I'm so proud of you!" I gasped when I finally came up for air.

I really was. I hadn't asked him to give up drinking, figuring he would know when and if he was ready. The delight I had felt when just three months after being free of Hyde he said he wanted to try, had been like no other.

Drinking had been a shield. His bratty, flirtatious nature had been armor. It was wonderful to see him slowly put them all aside and blossom into his true self.

"Tonight, I want to take your knot," said Eban, his eyes flashing silver.

Every thought I had ever had fell out of my mind as my cock swelled painfully against my fly.

"But... but," I babbled incoherently. I couldn't hurt him.

He saw my reluctance and scowled. "Have you seen the size of the toys I have been practicing with?"

I had. I had helped him practice with them. Happy memories flowed across my mind's eye. I groaned as pre-cum leaked out of me.

"Tonight will be perfect," continued Eban. "My hundred days, the divorce, and I'm pretty sure I will be ripe by tonight. The extra horniness will certainly help."

I groaned helplessly. "Okay," I croaked.

Eban beamed at me, rose up on his tiptoes to kiss my nose and then made to leave.

I made a strangled noise from deep in my throat. "Eban!" I pleaded. "You can't say all that and then just leave!"

He chuckled warmly as his eyes sparkled. Then he gave me an exaggerated sigh, as if he was hard done by, before dropping gracefully to his knees in front of me.

"Come on then," he said drolly.

I unzipped my fly and released my cock with a relieved groan. Life was very, very good.

Bonus Epilogue

Thank you for reading my book, I hope you enjoyed it!

Do you want to read Eban taking Bastion's knot?
Sign up to my newsletter for instant access to a **free bonus epilogue.**

If you are already a subscriber, don't worry! The link was in the November 14th 2022 newsletter.
(If you signed up after that, follow the link in your welcome email.)

Limited time offer Not one, but TWO free books when you sign up to my newsletter!

Sign up now and your welcome email will contain links to download your bonus epilogue & a free copy of Incubus Broken AND Omega Alone.

These books aren't on Kindle Unlimited, so grab them will you can.

How about exclusive short stories and opportunities to receive free copies of new releases before anyone else does?

Sign up for my newsletter.

https://www.srodman.net/newsletter-sign-up.html

It comes out once a month, you can unsubscribe at any time and I never spam, because we all hate spam.

If the link is broken, please type www.srodman.net into your browser.

Books By S. Rodman

All my books can be found on my Amazon Author page HERE

Or view at www.srodman.net

Darkstar Pack

Evil Omega

Evilest Omega

Evil Overlord Omega

Duty & Magic: MM Modern Day Regency

Lord Garrington's Vessel

Earl Hathbury's Vessel

The Bodyguard's Vessel

Hell Broken

Past Life Lover

How to Romance an Incubus

Lost & Loved

Dark Mage Chained

Prison Mated

Incubus Broken

Omega Alone

Printed in Great Britain
by Amazon